Edited by: Mel Noorderbroek at Write On Editorial

Cover design by: Cindy Ras

Paperback: 978-0-6458225-0-2

WATTLE IT BE?

THE WATTLE JUNCTION SERIES

*For everyone who takes a chance
and follows their dreams*

AUTHOR'S NOTE

Hi there!

Wattle It Be? is a small town, spicy friends-to-lovers romance written in Australian English so depending where in the world you're reading from there might occasionally be an 's' where you're expecting to see a 'z', along with a couple of other differences in spelling and slang.

Thanks so much for giving Wyatt and Billie's story a chance! I hope you love them as much as I do.

- Em

Trigger warning: sibling's death (not shown on page)

1

If Wyatt's memory was correct, he'd only agreed to host the charity bachelor auction at the Wattle Junction Hotel. Hell, he'd even waived the booking fee and donated a free night of accommodation to the silent auction. But the thing he hadn't done?

Volunteered to be auctioned.

He'd been rather adamant about that but still polite because his folks had raised him properly. Swallowing past the lump that formed in his throat whenever he thought about his parents, Wyatt focused on the two older women in front of him.

"Come on, Wyatt, darling, please?" Lulu Hampshire-James batted her eyelashes at him.

"No."

"Think of the children," she tried again, fiddling with the sparkly scarf she'd tied in her short hair.

"It's not going to work, ladies." He levelled the two matriarchs of Wattle Junction with a flat stare and waited. *Three, two, one ...*

"What would your grandmother say?" Joan Mandrill unloaded the biggest weapon in her arsenal: the guilt trip.

At least Lulu and Joan had the decency to look abashed about the sneaky tactic. Really, they needn't have worried. Nan would've been in cahoots with the two women he'd known since birth. Before her death five years ago, it had been rare to see his grandmother without her friends, caught up in a cloud of floral perfumes, their hands wrapped around something alcoholic and a twinkle in their eyes as they gossiped.

"My answer's still no." Wyatt brushed his chin length hair out of his face and tied half of it up, as he surveyed the function room. The extra tables had been assembled and his team was flittering around finalising place settings, arranging chairs.

"Told you," Teddy James muttered as he sped past, still in his sage Wattle Junction Hotel t-shirt and jeans. His long blond hair was in a man bun, but Wyatt was pretty sure his beard had been trimmed. His mother, Lulu's, work, no doubt. Wyatt and Teddy were regularly mistaken for brothers, which would've been funny, if it didn't always set off an ache in his chest when it happened.

Lulu leaned forward and beckoned for Wyatt to do the same. "You've grown into such a handsome, wonderful man. So kind and generous and community minded. Just like my boys."

Wyatt snorted. The inclusion of Lulu's four sons in the auction had surprised exactly no one. Even Owen was making the hour and a half trip out from Melbourne to take part. Then again, the James brothers were well known for being extra sweet to their mother about all the shenanigans she signed them up for. Wyatt was closest with the younger two, Teddy and Nate, but he couldn't think of a single bad thing to say about Rafferty or Owen either.

"We're trying to cater to every demographic, Wyatt. And you know the gruff, brooding type is always popular." Joan winked and Wyatt had to bite the inside of his cheek, so he didn't laugh.

"I think it's the tattoos, too. Gives you that bad boy edge. And don't worry about the bids. We've got a plan," she said.

These women always had a plan. That's how this ridiculous auction had started. How they'd managed to get a handful of men from the Wattle Junction Wallabies and local businesses to sign up was a mystery, though.

"Worst case scenario, you'll end up with me." Joan reapplied her bright pink lipstick. It matched her hair. Back when she'd been his primary school teacher, she'd been so serious. Wyatt never would've expected shy Mrs Mandrill to start a book club in her retirement and then campaign for every book to be a smutty romance. "I'm in charge of the back-up bids."

Well, that was a depressing thought. He hadn't actually considered that there'd be crickets when the bidding op— Wyatt shook his head. There'd be no bidding because he wasn't taking part, right?

"Although, I know of several young women and a few men who would be very happy to see your name added to the list."

Wyatt checked his watch. The rest of the cakes and treats for the dessert bar still had to be collected. "While I appreciate your offer—" he started, but Lulu shook her head and let out a loud sigh of resignation.

"Alright. We'll level with you."

That sounded ominous.

She fiddled with the stack of bracelets on her arm. "We

got a bit overconfident. Thought we'd be able to convince you."

Joan pulled a program out of her pink handbag and opened it. Wyatt's face was smack in the middle of the page.

"Oopsies." Lulu grinned.

"It'd look terrible if you backed out now." Joan didn't even attempt to keep the glee out of her voice. "Do it for your nan. She loved Kathleen's Place."

Wyatt sighed. Nan had loved the community home on the outskirts of Wattle Junction, and if she was alive, she'd have had him up on the stage with nothing more than a 'please, sweetheart'. Griffin would've thought it was a great laugh and probably insisted they do a two-for-one deal. Wyatt tugged at the collar of his T-shirt, pushing away the thought of his brother. He raised his eyebrows. "I'm not wearing a suit."

Lulu and Joan's smiles turned predatory.

"Or taking my shirt off," he clarified.

"What about suit but no tie? Something that says, 'I'm a casual guy'. Hints at rebellion. You're a modern-day James Dean with longer hair. If you don't have a suit ..." Lulu trailed off, awkwardness hanging in the air like the words she'd stopped herself from saying. Wyatt had a suit. A great one, even. He looked kick-ass in it, not that he'd ever admit that out loud. But the memories attached to it? There was nothing good there, and he'd never wear it again.

Wyatt gestured at his jeans, battered work boots and own sage green work shirt. "I'm wearing this."

"And a smile." Joan blew him a kiss while Lulu wrapped him up in a hug. Wyatt stiffened, his body not remembering what it was like to have loved ones around. He cleared his throat and made his excuses to leave, waiting until he was outside to draw in a deep breath and take a moment to let the heat of the summer afternoon warm his skin.

Wattle Junction was still home, even if he might be the last of his family to call it that.

It was purely coincidental that every time Billie saw Wyatt, she was all wet. At least that's what she told herself.

"Hi," she said, abandoning the sink full of dishes when he walked into the back room of the bakery her parents had owned forever.

He offered her one of his small smiles and peered down at the boxes filled with cupcakes, macaroons and slices decorated with tiny hearts and flowers. "You've outdone yourself."

Billie really did try not to notice how well his jeans hugged his ass, the denim moulded to the firm muscles she'd spent far too many hours imagining digging her fingers into as he moved above her ... and under her ... and behind her.

"The pub ready for tonight?" She cleared her throat, deciding that if she ignored the breathy pitch to her words, hopefully, Wyatt would too. Wiping her hands on her apron, Billie re-tied her light brown hair into a low ponytail.

"We're getting there." Something dark flickered across Wyatt's expression and Billie stepped forward.

"Everything okay?"

He scrubbed his hands down his face, scratching at his beard. His long fingers flexed and twisted in the dark brown hair and Billie swallowed a sigh. Some women hated beards on men, but she was firmly of the opinion that nothing tipped a guy from attractive to nuclear levels of hotness than some proper scruff on his cheeks. And Wyatt Andrews? He was the poster boy for testosterone and pure strength. But add in his soulful, deep chocolate eyes that hinted at a gentleness she wouldn't normally expect from someone so big? It was almost too much.

Just like his annoying ability to read a room and know exactly what everyone was thinking. Billie guessed it came with the territory considering he'd been a bartender for years. Although if he could *not* notice how flushed her skin was right now, that would be super helpful.

Another thing that would be great? If her sub-conscious could get the message that just because he smiled at her didn't mean he wanted to do very dirty things to her.

Here at the bakery.

In his office at the pub.

Anywhere, really.

Ever since her ex, Max, ended things six months ago because it was all 'getting too serious', something inside Billie had woken up and demanded she acknowledge the masculine perfection that was standing right in front of her. That observed things from behind his bar, a tiny smile pulling at the lips she desperately wanted to feel against her skin.

"... and now they've roped me in to it."

Shit. She'd blacked out for a minute there, lost in her fantasy of dragging Wyatt into her storeroom and sinking to her knees.

"Oh?" Billie said. And congratulated herself because really, even just breathing was a struggle right now and she'd managed to say something. Maybe next time she'd aim for multiple syllables, really shoot for the stars.

"Joan's going to bid on me if no one else does."

Hold. The. Phone.

"You're going to be in the auction?"

Wyatt's attractiveness tripled when he blushed. "Lulu and Joan got me in a weak moment."

Lulu and Joan deserved a goddamn medal. The keys to the city. Every accolade there was.

"You'll get plenty of bids."

Wyatt raised his eyebrows and shook his head. "Griffin would've been a better choice."

The mention of his brother had a sobering effect on her hormones and Billie straightened. Should she give him the picnic basket now? She never knew how to bring this up. But ignoring what day tomorrow would be was wrong, even if it was what Wyatt probably preferred.

Wyatt tapped his hand against the big bench in the middle of the room. "Anyway, I'd better get back there. Make sure everything's ready."

He started to stack the boxes onto the trolley he'd brought with him, and Billie rushed forward to help. Sod it. She'd give him the pies and cakes she'd made for him now rather than leaving them outside his door like she normally did.

"Wyatt?" The way his shoulders flattened told her that he knew what was coming next.

"You didn't have to do this," he said and the gruffness in his tone didn't offend her like it might have someone else.

"I know. But you shouldn't have to face this alone. It's just a little something to help you remember that we're all thinking of you and Griffin."

Losing Griffin had hit the whole town hard, but no one more so than Wyatt and his parents.

"He'd have been thirty this year."

"I know," she whispered, and Wyatt angled his face away

from hers so she couldn't see his expression. "He'd have been a great thirty-year-old."

Billie pretended she didn't notice Wyatt's sniff or know why he was undoing his hair, letting the chin-length strands fall around his face so he could hide behind them. Everyone grieved in different ways and Wyatt had chosen to do it privately. She—and the rest of Wattle Junction—wouldn't look for him at the pub tomorrow. Or expect to see him around town. He'd be somewhere else, doing whatever he needed, to get through his brother's birthday.

Billie waited until the trolley was fully loaded to pass him the small basket filled with things she knew he liked. She didn't say anything and neither did he.

She froze when Wyatt leaned forward. Billie was suddenly aware of how close they were standing, almost shoulder to shoulder, the scent of something spicy and enticing clinging to his body.

Wyatt's dark eyes met her light ones and his lips barely moved as he murmured his thanks. Billie was about to reply when he edged forward, dropping the most featherlight, blink-and-you'll-miss-it kiss on her cheek.

"I appreciate it," Wyatt said, and then he was gone.

2

———

Wyatt was leaning against the wall near the stage when a strong hand clapped his shoulder.

"Heard you put up a good fight, mate." Nate James grinned and offered him a beer. Wyatt declined because he never drank while working and despite what was about to happen, he *was* working.

"Hardly. I should've expected they'd pull a stunt like this. Your mum and Joan were quizzing me about dating the other day."

"An easy mistake," Teddy said, as he and Owen arrived. Both wore suits, although the difference between their appearances was laughable. Owen was polished and proper, all clean lines and classic colours. Exactly what someone would expect of a lawyer from the big city. Teddy, on the other hand, had chosen a pink jacket and apparently decided that buttoning his shirt was optional. He embodied the type of coolness Wyatt had never been able to muster up the effort to try and emulate.

"I don't think I've ever had a conversation with Mum or

Mrs Mandrill without being asked about the women in my life," Owen said dryly, before sipping his beer. "I mean, not since I left primary school. That would've been weird."

"What's weird is that you still insist on calling her 'Mrs Mandrill' like twenty years later," Teddy said, helping himself to the spare beer Nate had put on the high-top table next to them.

"Good of you all to volunteer, though." Wyatt stood up straighter, but it was pointless. Even Owen, the shortest of all the brothers at six one, was taller than him. Only by a smidge, but still.

If Wyatt was a betting man, he'd guess that Teddy would fetch the most money because it was impossible to dislike the guy. And the fact that he looked like a Viking made him very popular with all the women who visited the hotel.

"Volunteer is a bit of a stretch. I don't recall being asked." Nate laughed easily as he rolled up the sleeves of his grey business shirt. He'd forgone a jacket and his favourite pair of paint splattered Converse sneakers were on his feet. They all nodded hello as the oldest brother Rafferty stalked towards them, weaving through tables, his mobile glued to his ear.

"Whose idea was it to give Mum and Joan a microphone?" Rafferty asked, once he'd ended his call.

"They brought their own." The corners of Wyatt's mouth quirked up as everyone smiled.

"You've got to respect their community spirit," Owen said. "There's nothing they won't do for Kathleen's Place."

"Except neither of them are being auctioned off like a slab of meat." Teddy swallowed a sip of beer and winked. If anyone looked up flirt in the dictionary, Wyatt assumed there would be no definition. Just Teddy's picture.

"Not that I'm complaining," Teddy said.

"And what exactly will you be offering the lucky winner who purchases you?" Nate asked.

"Whatever they want." Teddy waggled his eyebrows. "Nothing boring like this loser." He pointed at Owen.

"Free legal advice is a good prize," Owen grumbled.

"It's supposed to be a date. Or have you forgotten what that is?" Teddy snickered and Owen ignored him, turning to Nate.

"What did you end up deciding on?"

"An art workshop and dinner here. Eloise said I could use the studio at Kathleen's Place."

"I bet she did," Teddy teased. "Because—"

Wyatt checked his phone but really he was hiding his smile. If there was ever a couple of friends who needed to open their eyes and see what was right in front of them, it was Nate and Eloise Hamilton, the social worker at Kathleen's Place.

Nate elbowed Teddy. "Because nothing, mate. Raff, you still doing the tour of the station?"

"Yep. Well, the bits they're allowed to see."

"What about you?" Owen asked Wyatt.

He scratched the back of his neck. "I haven't really thought about it."

There was a loud *tap, tap, tap* and Lulu's voice filled the room. "I hope everyone enjoyed their dinner. Can we have another round of applause for Wyatt and the wonderful team here at the Wattle Junction Hotel." She paused and Wyatt nodded, his left arm extending towards where the kitchen and wait staff were standing in the back of the room.

"Now, let's get this party started. We're so grateful to everyone who volunteered"—all the James brothers snorted in unison—"to be a part of our special bachelor auction! Let's kick it off by welcoming my oldest, Detective Rafferty

James to the stage." Teddy and Nate pushed Rafferty forward, snickering when he shook his head and trudged up the steps to where Lulu and Joan were. "For those who don't know, Raff's thirty-three, looks smashing in his uniform and he loves a full-bodied ... red wine!"

Gentle laughter rippled through the crowd before Joan interjected, "And he knows how to use a pair of handcuffs. Who wants to start the bidding?"

"Oh, Jesus," Owen muttered.

Wyatt probably should have swapped Joan's wine for something non-alcoholic a little bit earlier.

"This'll be good for him," Nate said. "Distract him from everything that went down with Cassie."

Wyatt wasn't close enough to Rafferty to ask about why he'd split up with his long-term girlfriend recently, but he'd certainly noticed the melancholy in the detective's eyes each time he came by the pub and at footy training.

"Who do you think will sell for the most?" Teddy asked as the bidding climbed steadily to two hundred dollars. Wattle Junction was a special place. Not just the standard small town where everyone knew everyone's business and newcomers weren't considered locals until they'd been there for several years. There was always a little bit of magic in the air, a sense of community spirit that bound all the residents together. Case in point: the two pies and small selection of cakes and desserts from Billie stashed upstairs in Wyatt's apartment on the top floor of the hotel.

It was no secret that tomorrow would be hard for him. It always was. More so now that his parents weren't here anymore either. But hopefully he'd speak to them tomorrow, maybe share some memories about Griffin and do his best to atone for everything he'd done that fateful day when they'd lost him.

A round of applause dragged Wyatt from his thoughts and he realised Owen was now on the stage, a wry expression on his face. No doubt Joan had said something equally inappropriate about him. Someone up the back opened the bidding with a loud "one hundred and fifty dollars!" which prompted several cat calls and if Wyatt wasn't mistaken, a pink tinge to spread across Owen's cheeks.

"You'll have to get used to all the attention, darling," Lulu said. "Can I tell them? Please?"

Sympathy coursed through Wyatt's veins when Owen pulled at his tie. Talk about being put on the spot.

"Owen's bought the old law office! He's coming home, folks!"

Excited chatter filled the room and Owen nodded, his mouth pulled tight into an odd combination of a grimace and a smile.

"All my boys will be home! And they're all single, ladies." Lulu winked.

Owen's return to Wattle Junction was great. But heat crept up Wyatt's spine, pulling all his muscles tight. The chatter of the crowd faded, and he blinked. Tried to focus on what Teddy, Nate and Rafferty were saying but blood rushed through his veins, pounding loudly between his ears. He excused himself quickly, mumbling some nonsense about checking on the kitchen and promising to be back before it was his turn to be auctioned.

Because the James family's exciting news was just another reminder that his brother was never coming back.

And it was all Wyatt's fault that he and his parents never got to say goodbye.

BILLIE FOUND Wyatt in his office, sitting on his desk next to a pile of papers and three empty coffee cups. Light spilt through the partially open door, highlighting his profile and casting shadows under his eyes. She paused, one hand resting on the doorframe. Maybe she should just leave him be. Let him have this quiet moment he so clearly needed. Then she remembered how fast he'd hightailed it out of the function room, his chin practically touching his chest.

"Hey," she said.

Wyatt didn't look up, his shoulders still curled forward. "I'll be out in a second," he mumbled. His voice was heavy and dull. How long had it been since she'd heard the old jokey lilt that everyone associated with Wyatt. The way he'd ask 'what'll it be' from behind the bar, eyes crinkling, his big grin automatic.

Too long, Billie decided.

Normally, she would have backed away, but something stopped her. She could try to convince herself it was her conscience. That she was just being neighbourly and upholding the unwritten rule everyone in Wattle Junction lived by: to look after each other. But it was more than that. It was guilt. And—she swallowed—selfishness. Because she'd been trapped in limbo with Wyatt for what felt like forever.

"I'm sorry if I made it worse," she said. Even with the buzz from the function room slipping down the hall, Billie's words were still too loud in the dark office.

"You didn't make it worse." Wyatt's tone was gruff, the muscles in his jaw and neck working overtime as he swallowed.

"Wyatt—"

"I'll be out in a minute, Billie, okay?"

Her shoulders dropped and she stared at the dark

carpet under her feet. Now wasn't the time to try and make things right. Any fool could see that. And Billie was a fool. Because Wyatt was never going to see her as anything other than the first girl who broke his brother's heart.

NOT EVEN THE sight of Teddy James strutting around the stage, his shirt off and muscles gleaming under the lights could pull a smile from Billie. She dropped into her seat, suspicion curling through her belly when her parents snapped their mouths shut, guilty expressions on their faces.

"What?"

"Nothing." Her mother, Daphne, folded her serviette and then straightened her knife and fork. A quick glance at her father, Ben, revealed he was burying his nose in his phone, scrolling through his emails so fast that there was no way he was actually reading them. He also wasn't wearing his glasses. When Billie thought about it, her parents had been behaving strangely for the last few days. She'd interrupted several of their conversations and they'd fallen silent or changed the subject.

"What's going on?"

They exchanged a look. The kind that doubled as an unspoken conversation for a couple who had been together for over thirty years.

"We'll talk about it tomorrow." Daphne tried to squeeze her hand but Billie shook her off. Her eyes narrowed and she crossed her arms.

"I don't want to talk about it tomorrow."

With a heavy sigh, Ben reached for Daphne's hand and

she nodded. "We've been thinking it's time to retire. Hand the bakery over to you."

"Nothing's set in stone," Daphne rushed to add.

Billie stared down at the half-eaten chicken and pesto pasta dish on her plate. It was her favourite but after everything with Wyatt, and now this, her appetite had officially gone home.

The bakery had always been a part of her life. So much so that none of the Winnicks were capable of sleeping in. She'd spent countless afternoons there after school, helping her parents bag up unsold stock to be dropped off at Kathleen's Place or friends' places.

There had never been a question about what Billie would do when she finished school because this wasn't the first time her parents had mentioned that she could take it over. Make it hers. But she'd kind of thought that was years away and lately—she swallowed—she'd been having doubts about staying there forever.

Every day Billie got up and did the same things in the same order. There was no excitement. No spark. Taking on even more responsibility—all the responsibility—at the bakery would leave even less time for what she truly loved doing. Baking was in her blood. The call to create things, especially celebration cakes and specialty desserts, for those she loved was a fire inside of Billie that she couldn't ever imagine being extinguished.

"What do you think?" Daphne had to raise her voice as a raucous round of applause filled the room, a blonde in a tight dress rushing on to the stage to wrap her arms around Teddy. Someone was very happy with her purchase.

"Billie?" Daphne asked again.

If she didn't step up and take over, her parents would be so disappointed. This had always, *always* been the plan.

Panic zapped through Billie's body. She didn't know what to think.

Actually, that wasn't true. Deep down Billie was pretty sure she knew exactly what she wanted. But verbalising it? She'd allowed herself to file it in the too hard basket for far too long.

Billie had to stand up for herself, for her future. In life and in love. *Oh, shit.* She was literally standing up. Billie ignored the startled looks of her parents and the strange hush that had fallen over the room.

Wyatt was on the stage, still in his jeans and Wattle Junction Hotel shirt, hair all mussed like he'd been running his hands through it. Their gazes met across the crowded room and he raised his eyebrows ever so slightly.

"Who—" Joan didn't even get to finish her question before the words burst out of Billie's mouth.

"Five hundred dollars!"

3

S olitude was what Wyatt needed today. Time alone with his thoughts. The sounds of nature. A warm breeze as he hiked through the trails of the Wattle Valley.

It had taken him a while to figure out what he should do on the anniversary of Griffin's birth and death. Because only Griffin could pull off the unthinkable and leave this earth on his birthday. A final selfless act to help his family after he was gone. Like if there was only one day instead of a birthday and death day, it would be easier for them. But nothing changed the fact that the hole he'd left behind in all their hearts would never heal.

Wyatt stopped, letting summer heat seep into his skin. He hadn't seen anyone all day, which was exactly what he wanted. Bird song filled the air as he started walking again. The scuff of his hiking boots against the ground was familiar and comforting. He adjusted the straps of his backpack and dropped his gaze as he crested the final ascent to the clearing where he was planning to spend the afternoon. Wyatt never liked to be overwhelmed and seeing the wide, open space from his brother's favourite lookout always stole his breath. It was a visceral reminder that the world was still so big even if Wyatt's version had irrevocably changed four years ago. A different person would've thrown themselves into championing research into undiagnosed aneurysms.

But that wasn't who Wyatt was.

He wasn't a leader. He was the everyday guy. Who got all the little stuff done so the big picture magic could happen. When his parents had wanted to run away from Wattle Junction, from all the memories that should've brought them comfort but were still too confronting, Wyatt had come up with their escape plan. He'd stay and run the pub while they did a few laps of Australia; until they could face coming home.

Wyatt kept his gaze on the ground that was littered with gumnuts, twigs and little rocks. Told himself to take a deep breath before he raised his head and looked across the valley properly. His worries could fill the vast space in front of him and Wyatt would allow himself to wallow, to contemplate all the things that stopped him from sleeping properly. Just for a second. Out here no one could see him fall apart. Then he'd go back to being strong.

What if my parents can never forgive me?

What if they leave me forever, too?

He pulled his phone out of his backpack and ignored all the text messages that he knew would be waiting. As one of the last people on the planet who refused to have anything to do with social media, Wyatt only used his mobile for its original purpose. He checked the time and opened FaceTime, frowning at his own reflection in the little square. The flat line of his lips was so severe. Sleep had totally eluded him last night—not uncommon given the significance of today—but he couldn't deny there had also been another reason.

Billie.

Why did I kiss her on the cheek as a thank you for the little treats she made me?

Why did she buy me at the auction?

Wyatt pushed all his thoughts about the woman who filled his dreams most nights aside and hit call. Best to get this done. Shame washed over him. Everyone grieved in different ways. Who was he to judge his parents for running away? It rang and rang before going to his dad's voicemail. There was the same response from his mum's number.

Wyatt blinked back a few tears and pushed his sunglasses up into his hair. Told himself that it didn't mean anything that they didn't answer. They were probably out for their own walk. Or had forgotten to take their phones off silent. A cool breeze rolled across the lookout. If Wyatt believed in signs, he'd have thought it was Griffin. Telling him to stop overthinking everything and that there was nothing he could've done that fateful day. He wasn't being punished for what had happened.

But it would be a lie.

BILLIE HAD ALWAYS THOUGHT that one of Teddy's superpowers was never looking stressed. It was a trait he shared with all his brothers.

"Thank God you're here," Teddy called before she'd even closed the pub's front door behind her.

Billie cocked her head to the side, her gaze sweeping across the busy dining room.

She and Teddy were friends, but he'd never sent her an SOS text out of the blue before.

"The kitchen staff have all called in sick and Tony can't stay. He's got his kids. Do you have any pies left from today? Or rolls?"

Oh, damn. Today was the one day of the year that they needed everything to run smoothly. "Does Wyatt know?"

"I don't want to call him unless I have to. Mum and Dad are coming. So are my brothers. Tony's whipping up a bunch of lasagnes and a jumbo curry. If we can add some stuff from the bakery, we could call it a fixed menu and muddle through."

Luckily, there was a box of unsold pasties and pies sitting on the backseat of Billie's car. Kathleen's Place would have to go without today.

Billie tied her hair into a ponytail. "I'll grab the pies and then help Tony in the kitchen. Get him to show me how to use the fryers. Everything's better with hot chips or wedges."

She ducked behind the bar and stowed her handbag under the counter next to Teddy's uni bag.

"Thanks for not calling Wyatt, especially considering it's ..." She didn't know how to describe it. His dark day? The day he disappeared?

"Speaking of Wyatt ..."

Teddy wasn't the first person to ask her about what had happened last night. Everyone who'd come into the bakery today had wanted a delicious treat with a side of piping hot tea about what was going on between Billie and the broody bartender. Probably that was something she should have considered before she showed all her cards at the auction.

"I don't want to talk about it."

Teddy snickered. "I can guarantee that answer's not going to fly with my mum."

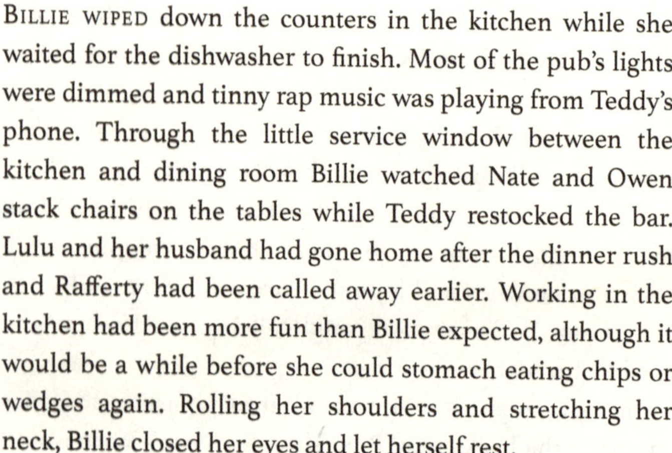

BILLIE WIPED down the counters in the kitchen while she waited for the dishwasher to finish. Most of the pub's lights were dimmed and tinny rap music was playing from Teddy's phone. Through the little service window between the kitchen and dining room Billie watched Nate and Owen stack chairs on the tables while Teddy restocked the bar. Lulu and her husband had gone home after the dinner rush and Rafferty had been called away earlier. Working in the kitchen had been more fun than Billie expected, although it would be a while before she could stomach eating chips or wedges again. Rolling her shoulders and stretching her neck, Billie closed her eyes and let herself rest.

When she opened them, the first thing she noticed was the bins near the rear door. *Right. Back to work.*

Even though February evenings were still warm, it was significantly cooler outside than it had been inside the kitchen. Billie tossed the rubbish and leaned against the brick exterior sucking in a deep breath that didn't smell like butter chicken curry.

"Billie?" Wyatt said. He stepped out from behind his car. She'd been so out of it she hadn't realised his green 4WD was parked in its usual spot. "Why did you come out of the kitchen? What are you doing here?"

Ahhh. This didn't look good, did it? The night after she basically forced him into a date, and she was hanging around his business. Wearing a Wattle Junction Hotel apron. Billie cringed. She'd committed to putting herself out there, but a girl needed time to get organised. To really gauge Wyatt's interest. Just because she'd caught him looking at her a few times and he always came to the bakery to collect the hotel's orders didn't actually mean he was interested in her. She could hope it did, but hope wasn't anything without action to back it up.

Billie chose her words carefully. "There was a small hiccup with the kitchen service tonight."

"What?" Wyatt moved forward and the outdoor light illuminated the confusion on his face. There was something else, too. Fatigue, she realised. His hair was tied back but several strands had escaped, the ends curling and framing his face. A hint of sunburn kissed his nose and cheeks.

"Everyone called in sick. But don't worry. Teddy handled it."

Wyatt dragged a hand across the front of his shirt as if he was brushing off some dust or dirt. The movement made his bicep flex and call to her.

"Why didn't anyone ring me?" If she'd had to predict this moment, Billie would have expected Wyatt to be gruff, maybe even a little annoyed but his tone was gentle, almost ... *broken.*

"We knew you needed space today. Honestly. It's not a big deal. A few friends pitching in."

His eyes darkened when she said 'friends'. Shit. She might not know what her plan was, but Billie didn't want to be just friends with Wyatt, even if their history was complicated. Griffin's face flashed into her mind. Okay. More than complicated.

"Thank you."

Relief flooded through her, and Billie sagged back against the brick wall. The rough edges scratched at her bare arms, but she didn't notice. Wyatt wasn't mad. Thank God. The last thing anyone wanted was to make today even harder for him.

"You're welcome."

He moved towards the door. "I should help pack up."

"Or …" she said and Wyatt stopped, turning to look at her. His body was so close the warmth of his skin taunted her. "You could just go upstairs. No one's expecting you in there. I won't tell anyone. This can be our little secret."

Wyatt shook his head slowly and Billie knew what he was going to say before the words even left his mouth.

"Secrets are never a good idea."

4

____

This family dinner wasn't just a family dinner. That much was apparent as soon as Billie sat down at the scarred walnut table that held the marks of her childhood. There were splotches from the paint pens she'd been far too casual with when she shook them. The permanent ink staining the wood no matter how hard her parents had tried to get it off. Scratches from where her tub of slime had cracked, the gooey mixture gluing itself to the table and needing to be scraped off.

Tonight, however, it was covered in her favourite treats. A big tray of charcuterie and cheeses. Three types of dips, all vibrant colours, a little rainbow amongst olives and cherry tomatoes. And because the Winnicks were bakers, there was focaccia and a pull apart cheese and bacon scroll that everyone knew Billie would reach for first.

"I thought we'd keep it simple tonight. It's too hot to turn the oven on," Daphne said as she filled three wine glasses with a sauvignon blanc that Billie would bet came from New Zealand.

Sweat dotted Billie's brow and she wiped it away with the back of her hand. "It should be cooler tomorrow."

Banal chit chat was *not* usually the conversation of choice for the Winnicks.

"We wanted to apologise," Ben said.

"We never should have dropped that bomb on you the other night," Daphne agreed.

Billie tugged a piece of the pull apart free, needing to do something with her hands. "I just wasn't expecting it. I didn't know you were thinking of retiring soon." For a family that spent all their work days together, it seemed ridiculous that the topic had never come up. That was a reflection on her own missteps, as well as her parents'.

"Still. We should have chosen our moment better." Daphne helped herself to some brie and spicy salami.

Billie paused mid-chew. The delicious cheesy-bacon bread sat like lead in her stomach.

"You let us know when you're ready and we can start planning for the changeover."

Billie swallowed and tried to find the right way to tell her parents that she wasn't sure this would be the right move for her.

"There's no one else we'd want the bakery to go to," Ben said. "We're so proud of you, Billie."

Well, damn.

IT WAS A SHORT WALK—LIKE everything in Wattle Junction— back to Billie's tiny cottage. Her place wasn't fancy, but it was home. One day she'd paint the weatherboards and update the bathroom so it wasn't coral. Make a serious dent in the list of things she wanted to do.

Living with her parents until she was twenty-four had been *interesting,* but it had allowed her to save every spare dollar until she could scrounge together the deposit for the two-bedroom cottage on a tiny plot of land. There wasn't much of a garden, just some daisies that the previous owner had planted. Eventually she planned to add a peach or cherry tree. Something to give her fruit that she could use in her baking.

If I'm still baking.

Having her future blasted so wide open made her head pound. Shouldn't she be sure of what she wanted to do by now?

Or be brave enough to commit to the bakery?

Or know how to make it clear to Wyatt that she was interested in him? And that she was so much more than his brother's ex-girlfriend? That it would be okay if they were to cross the line from friends to something more. Griffin had been gone for years now, and they'd been over long before that.

But still Wyatt waited. Kept her at arm's length. Acted like he'd be dishonouring his brother if he acted on the heat that always sprung up between them.

She flopped down on the rocking chair on her small porch and tilted her face towards the fading sunlight.

The solution for one of her problems was simple. She just had to figure out what kind of date would prove to Wyatt that it would be okay for him to give them a chance.

A new bra and some sexy panties that made her feel amazing wouldn't hurt either.

Just in case.

This wasn't a big deal.

If anything, it was just good manners. A simple thank you for stepping in when he couldn't. Was Wyatt's decision to deliver it under the cover of darkness intentional? Well, yes. But every resident of a small town knew even the trees had eyes. If word got out that he was visiting Billie's house, there'd be talk. Even more than there already was after the auction.

Wyatt walked down her driveway, his steps quickening when the security light above the car port switched on. A few mosquitoes buzzed around the globe.

He shifted his weight from one foot to the other and dragged his free hand through his hair as the sweet smell of the roses he was carrying filled his senses.

What had he been thinking? This was a mistake. And roses? Everyone knew they were romantic flowers. Even if he hadn't chosen any red ones. People rarely gave each other roses unless it meant something more. He could try to convince Billie—and himself—that just because they'd come from his roof top garden it meant something different. Something harmless and neighbourly but even the thought left a bitter taste in his mouth. Why hadn't he just picked up a bottle of Billie's favourite wine and left it on her doorstep with a note?

The voice that whispered in his mind made him close his eyes, grind his jaw together.

It was like Griffin was right behind him, whispering, *"because you wanted to see her."*

He shook his head, but the whispers persisted. *"And you chose roses because you know they're her favourite."*

Just like Wyatt knew she hated blueberry muffins and thought cricket was the dullest sport ever invented. She wore floral dresses with fluttery skirts whenever she was feeling fancy but was just as happy in denim cut-offs and a singlet. She'd order cocktails on girls' nights out but preferred a glass of wine. Anything sour would make her lips pucker and her nose wrinkle adorably. Her fair skin always made him want to press his fingers into it, see the contrast against his own olive complexion.

But none of that changed the most important fact: she could never be Wyatt's when she'd belonged to Griffin.

Wyatt placed the roses on the rocking chair next to the door and hurried away before anyone—including Billie—could see him.

They'd go to dinner and then that would be it. He'd keep his distance. Stay away from the woman his brother had always regretted letting go.

THE NEXT MORNING, Wyatt woke up with a thumping headache and a sore neck. An empty whiskey glass sat on the small table next to the outdoor couch. He blinked as early morning rays of sunshine tried to blind him. There had been a moment last night when he distinctly remembered trying to force himself to go to bed. But the stars had called to him, convincing him to stay in the balmy evening air. Not a hard decision when all that waited for him downstairs was an empty apartment.

Wyatt sat up and stretched, felt his muscles loosen as he tried to push away the heaviness of a restless night of sleep. After stomping down the stairs, rushing through a shower and a bowl of cornflakes, he found himself behind the bar brewing a cup of his favourite medium roast. His parents still hadn't called, a fact that clouded his already heavy mind. He'd had even less contact with them lately and it was starting to feel intentional.

A knock at the door distracted him. When Wyatt opened the heavy wooden door, Billie was standing there with the day's pastries.

"I was just about to come and get them," he said in greeting before taking the box from her.

"I know," she said brightly. Too brightly. A second glance at Billie made his heart pound. Her eyes were red, her lips extra pink today.

She'd been crying.

"Hey," he murmured. "You okay?"

"I'm fine." The crack in her voice made him frown.

"You don't look fine."

Billie sniffled and Wyatt couldn't stop himself from adding, "I mean, you look good. You always look good."

Even if Wyatt wouldn't allow himself to act on the thoughts that filled his mind and dreams—another reason he was so damn grumpy today—there was no way he was letting her stand in front of him and cry. Not without offering her some comfort. He put the box on the mahogany bar and turned back towards her. Billie hadn't moved and she was blinking furiously.

"Hey, hey," Wyatt said, after flicking the front door lock. He reached for her hands and led her over to one of the tables, ignoring the heat that burned where their palms met. "What's going on?"

Billie took a deep, shuddering breath. "Nothing. Honestly. I'm fine."

The word 'baby' was on the tip of Wyatt's tongue but he swallowed it, sitting down opposite her. "Billie."

She shook her head and wiped her eyes.

"Do you want a coffee? Or something stronger? I know

the bartender here," he joked. Some of the tension in his chest loosened when Billie offered him a watery laugh.

"Do you ever feel like a total disappointment to your parents?"

Please. She was looking at the president of that club. This time it was his voice that wavered. "I do."

"Mum and Dad want to retire." She pushed her hair off her face. "And I realised this morning when I was slicing the millionth loaf of bread that I've probably made there that I don't want to do this for the rest of my life. I've been thinking it for a while but trying to ignore that I'd have to actually tell them."

"Ah."

"They've spent all this time building their business and now that it's time for me to step up so they can step down, I don't want to do it. How ungrateful can I be? Please don't tell anyone."

The irony of Billie asking Wyatt to keep a secret wasn't lost on him. These walls held so many secrets it was a miracle the hotel wasn't sinking into the ground.

"I don't want to hurt their feelings."

Her words set off a familiar ache in Wyatt's chest. Not wanting to hurt people's feelings was exactly why he'd never acted on his feelings for Billie. But this wasn't about him. And if all they could ever be was friends, then he'd be a good one to her now, which meant she deserved the truth. Luckily, the Winnicks had a very different relationship to his with his parents. "I'm sure they just want what's best for you."

Billie nodded and fidgeted in her seat. The blinds were still closed but slices of sunlight slipped through the gaps painting an ethereal backdrop behind her. She was so beautiful.

And so far out of his reach.

"I know that. I really do. But how can I tell them that I don't want the business when I don't know if I'm brave enough to go after what I actually want."

"You just have to be honest with them. Easier said than done, I know."

"Being an adult sucks," she whispered.

A smile pulled at the corner of Wyatt's mouth. "Yep."

"Okay." Billie shook her hands in front of her and then pulled her hair into a ponytail. "I've taken up enough of your time. Thanks for listening."

"Any time."

Neither spoke on the short walk to the door but Billie paused after Wyatt had unlocked it and opened it. "Thanks for the flowers, too."

It took Wyatt a minute to process her words. How had she known they were from him? Like the coward that he was, he'd pocketed the note he'd written and just left the flowers.

"You wrapped them in a Wattle Junction Hotel tea towel."

Ah. Well, that was okay. One less secret for him to keep. Friends could give each other flowers. "You're welcome."

"Are you free on Sunday night?" Billie asked.

"Uhhh ..."

"You owe me a dinner," she murmured.

Right, the auction. "You're happy with just a dinner?" Wyatt asked, remembering that the James brothers had talked about their dates including an activity. Was that what Billie expected?

"It's a start." A soft smile graced her lips and before Wyatt had a chance to figure what it meant, Billie had slipped out the door.

5

S haved and moisturised legs? Check.

A glass of wine to calm Billie's nerves? Check.

A spritz of perfume right between her breasts? Why the hell not. She *was* hoping to give Wyatt the nudge he needed to see her differently.

Maybe she'd have another glass of wine. Just a small one.

Billie tossed her head, shook out the curls she'd added to her naturally wavy hair. Men would never truly appreciate how much effort went into looking natural. A swipe of her favourite peach lip gloss and she was ready.

She was locking her front door when she heard footsteps on her gravel drive.

Please don't be Wyatt cancelling.

"Billie," Max called. Her shoulders tensed. What did her ex-boyfriend want?

"Do you have a minute?"

"Not really." Billie stashed her keys in the small gold clutch her mother had given her for Christmas.

"It'll just take a second." Which was how Billie and

Max's sex life could have been described. What had she been thinking dating him for a whole year?

Billie crossed her arms. "What's up, Max?"

It hadn't been a bad break up. Exactly zero tears had been shed when Max told her that he just couldn't see himself settling down any time soon. Because Billie hadn't wanted to marry him either. His company was ... *inoffensive*. God. She was so mad at past Billie for ever accepting the paltry relationship Max had offered her. Not that she was blameless. She could've been honest with herself about what ... *or who* ... she really wanted.

"You look great." His gaze dropped to the deep vee of her neckline. It was lower than she normally wore but damn it, her boobs looked great, and she wanted Wyatt to notice them. Notice her.

"Thanks."

"Don't worry. I'm not here to try and get you back," Max laughed lightly.

She raised her eyebrows and waited. Resisted the urge to make a 'hurry up' motion with her hands when Max took a deep breath and offered her a shy smile. Billie looked at him properly. His blond hair was longer than normal which made him appear younger than his thirty-five years. His face was relaxed, maybe even a bit *sheepish*?

"I'm getting married."

"Oh," she gasped, unable to stop herself. Because what the hell?

Max scratched the back of his neck. "Uh, yeah. So, I met someone and they're great. Not that you're not great. Because you are. Really great. We're just not great together. I mean you and me. My fiancée and I are really great together." Max blew out a loud, noisy breath. "I've got to stop saying great," he muttered, which made Billie smile.

"Congratulations," she said, really meaning it. Max was correct. They hadn't been right for each other and if he'd managed to find someone he loved enough to marry only six months after they'd split up?

That was ... *great.*

It was exactly what she was hoping to do with Wyatt, wasn't it? Not marry the guy. No, not that. Well, maybe in time. But Billie was so ready to move on. She couldn't be mad at Max for doing the same thing.

"I'm really happy for you." She reached forward and squeezed his hand.

"Would you be able to do me a teeny, tiny favour?" Max tossed her the puppy dog eyes she'd found so hard to resist when they first met.

"Uh ..."

"Would you make our wedding cake for us? No one makes better cakes than you do. Everyone in Wattle Junction always says so."

Billie's phone buzzed, reminding her that she needed to leave now. "Sure," she laughed. "I'll make your cake for you but I've got to go. I've got a date."

"With Wyatt?"

"How'd you know?"

"Oh." Max dragged his sneaker through the gravel at his feet. "The auction."

Right. The auction.

"And I always thought maybe you had a thing for him."

Billie sighed. She'd been a rotten girlfriend, too. She said goodbye to Max, promising to call to get the details for the cake in the next few days. It was time to go and get her man.

∼

IT WASN'T LIKE this was a real date.

God. When was the last time Wyatt actually went on a date? He racked his brain. He wasn't a recluse. There had been women. Beautiful, sexy women who'd recognised exactly what he was offering. A good time between the sheets without any commitment. Wyatt hadn't been in a place to give anything more.

But Billie was different. For so many reasons.

Which is why this isn't a real date, he reminded himself.

It was a casual hang out. *Damn.* It wasn't that either. *That* was how he'd categorised the fun he'd occasionally had with the other women. Wyatt opened the fridge and let the cool air wash over him but it did nothing to calm his nerves.

Here he was. Thirty-one years old and second guessing every choice he'd made about this night. Billie had suggested dinner downstairs but the idea of sitting in a fishbowl had sent Wyatt in a different direction.

Which he was now realising was far too intimate.

For God's sake. Wyatt had literally just finished lighting several candles. They were citronella to try and keep the mozzies away but *still.* And the vase of flowers on the table on the roof? What did it matter if he'd cut a few more roses to make the table look nice? He looked down at his jean-clad legs. He'd picked his good non-work pair because all the others were in the wash. No other reason.

Mercifully, Griffin's voice in his mind stayed silent.

Cracking open a beer, Wyatt caught his reflection in the mirrored splashback his mother had insisted on installing when they remodelled the kitchen. Should he trim his beard really quick? There was a delicate balance between rugged and full-on mountain man.

He was still debating it when there was a knock on his door.

FOR SOMEONE who wasn't on a date, Wyatt was having a lot of trouble not staring at Billie's ass as she ascended the stairs to the roof in front of him. She was wearing one of those swishy dresses he loved, and the material danced enticingly around her thighs. All that smooth skin taunted him.

"I had no idea this was up here," Billie said. Most people had the same reaction to the roof top space and garden. It spanned the whole top of the building and served several different purposes. The back wall of the covered area held a vertical garden with all the herbs the kitchen used. His mother's prized roses grew in huge black pots on the other side where they were partially protected from the elements. There was a long low table between the two outdoor couches, a citronella candle flickering in the middle of it.

He knew the moment that Billie spotted the rose bushes because she spun on her heels, her dress lifting with the motion and revealing another sliver of creamy thighs. "Wait. You grew the flowers you gave me?"

"I did. Can you imagine the fuss if I'd bought them from Swift's?" At the mention of the general store next to the pub, the light in Billie's eyes dimmed before her shoulders straightened, her chin jerking forwards.

"Hate to break it to you but I'm fairly certain Lulu saw me head up the stairs when I arrived. I've never met someone who could jump to conclusions quicker than her." Billie tucked her hair behind her ear and Wyatt's fingers itched to pull it loose just so he could do that for her.

"Gossip *is* hard to avoid here." Why did it sound like he was severely dehydrated?

"Does that make you nervous?" Billie asked.

Wyatt attempted a joke. "Anyone who's not scared of

Lulu and Joan and their crew is an idiot. Just ask the James brothers. They're probably planning our wedding," his voice hitched as he imagined Billie in a long dress, roses in her hair, promising to love him forever, "just because we're having dinner."

Billie sauntered towards him, her eyes never leaving his. The determination in her jaw and defiant posture was new. Wyatt swallowed.

"Well, if everyone's already jumping to assumptions, maybe we should give them something to really talk about?"

She stopped in front of Wyatt and reached for the buttons on her dress, right between her breasts.

6

____

Men liked ballsy women, right? The type that oozed confidence and weren't afraid to go after what they wanted. So why was Wyatt standing there looking like someone had smacked him across the face with whatever fish was on the specials board downstairs?

Her fingers caught around the third button. Should she stop? Run away and relocate to Mars?

"Billie." Wyatt's tortured tone was mimicked by his body language, the way his large hands scrubbed at his face, twisted in his hair. "We shouldn't."

That was ... not technically a no. A little spark of hope flickered to life in Billie's chest. She edged closer to Wyatt, watched him swallow thickly. "Why not?"

Please don't say because of Griffin. Please don't say because of Griffin.

"It wouldn't be right because of ..."

Billie steeled herself for the word that she knew was going to fall from Wyatt's full, totally kissable lips.

"... Griffin."

"I disagree." *Oh, shit.* Turns out she was a really ballsy woman.

"We should have dinner."

"I'd like to have you for dinner." Okay, so pre-gaming with two glasses of wine might've loosened Billie's tongue a touch too much. She'd felt the heat of his gaze as they climbed the stairs, and noticed how he tracked her movements as she explored the roof, his eyes lingering on the swell of her breasts. If he liked that, he was really going to like what she had on underneath.

"Billie."

She huffed out a long sigh. "Griffin and I were never right for each other. Max and I were never right for each other. Shall I continue?" It'd be great if Wyatt just agreed because listing her exes to the man she wanted so badly she could practically taste it? Not part of her plan.

"I've made a lot of mistakes in the past—" Wyatt started and where, where was this going?

"—and that's what this would be?" She cut in, painfully aware of the way her dress gaped open. How exposed she was.

"Yes," Wyatt nodded. The movement was jerky, unnatural. The man was looking everywhere but at her.

"You can't know that. I think you're scared. It's okay to want something just for yourself, Wyatt." Clearly the connection between her mouth and brain was broken because this confident, domineering version of herself had come out of nowhere. "I dare you to kiss me."

"We're not twelve." Wyatt laughed but the edges of his words were bitter, defeated. "My brother kissed you when he was twelve."

"And when he was thirteen." There was no denying her

and Griffin's past. "But we were kids. It was barely even a teenage romance."

"He always said that he regretted letting you go, especially towards the end."

"Probably because he had a serious case of rose-coloured glasses after everything went south with his ex. Griffin was a great guy. And I really cared for him. But we were kids and it was so long ago. Even if he was still here, I wouldn't want him. Not that way. When he died"—Wyatt flinched and regret coursed through Billie's body, but this had to be said—"I lost a friend. Nothing more. Griffin never made me feel the way you do."

Wyatt's swallow was noticeable. "How do I make you feel?"

"Wanted."

Fire flared in his eyes, but Wyatt didn't move, which was fine. Billie would go to him. One last time. But then he had to give her something. Prove she wasn't alone in this. Her heels clicked across the tiles.

"How do I make you feel, Wyatt?" Billie reached for his hands.

"Wanted," he whispered, right before he stepped backwards. "But I can't. I'm so sorry, Billie."

It took Wyatt ten seconds to realise what an enormous mistake he'd made. Billie was on the stairs, moving like she regularly ran in high heels. Maybe she did? He was fooling himself if he thought he knew everything about her. How would that be possible when he'd always held her at arm's length because of some misguided loyalty to his brother.

Like denying his true feelings would balance out his mistakes.

Griffin was gone forever.

His parents were gone. Maybe forever. They still hadn't bothered to call him back. Proving that people could be ghosts even before they died.

And he'd just told the one person who never failed to show up for him that he couldn't be with her. He'd essentially doomed himself to a life on his own, and what was the point of that? It wouldn't bring Griffin back. In fact, it would piss his brother off. A lot.

Wyatt wasn't trapped. He was refusing to move.

Fuck. He was a massive idiot.

He sprinted down the stairs, following the sounds of her heels. With each step, his heart pounded harder.

"Billie!" he called but she didn't stop. She didn't even turn around, which was exactly what he deserved.

He tried again but Billie sped up, rushing through the back area of the ground floor and bursting into the dining room. Of course, it was full. A hush fell over the crowd as Wyatt finally caught up with her.

"Please stop," he begged.

"It's fine, Wyatt. I just want to go home."

"Everything okay?" Teddy called from behind the bar and Wyatt nodded, his gaze never leaving Billie's eyes. They were full of hurt. That he'd put that there. *Fuck.* He had to fix this.

"Your dress," he whispered. It was still undone and now everyone could see her pink bra with lace around the edges.

"Oh my God." Billie's shoulders curled forward, and she hastily buttoned her top together with shaking fingers. When Wyatt stepped towards her, she flinched.

"Don't. It's fine. This isn't what it looks like," she called to the packed room. "And I'd really appreciate it if we could all agree to never mention this. At least not to my face." Her attempt at a laugh fell flat and Wyatt hated himself even more.

"Wonderful. Well, I'll be going now." Billie strode towards the big double doors, shoulders straight but her trembling hands gave her away.

Billie had put herself out there and taken a chance. Didn't Wyatt owe it to her—and himself—to do that, too? To be brave and honest? Besides it wasn't like everyone in Wattle Junction didn't know what had happened to his brother. Just because he'd been pretending that everything was fine didn't mean anyone had bought the act he'd tried so hard to sell. A quick glance around the room confirmed his suspicions. Concern and pity were etched on the faces of the people who'd done their best to hold him up and help him settle into his horrendous new normal. But the life he'd condemned himself to was farcical.

Billie pulled the door open.

Wyatt would never forgive himself if he didn't stop her. Be brave for her. For Griffin. For *himself*.

"The day Griffin died; he called me. Said he wasn't feeling good. I thought he was hungover because we'd had a birthday party for him the night before with a few mates." Wyatt paused and took a long steadying breath that did nothing to help his nerves.

"Mum, Dad and I were in Melbourne visiting a supplier. They wanted to come back straight away but it was me who said we should stay and finish the visit. It was for the renovation of the accommodation. Mum had this vision of how she wanted it to look, and I was sick of going to Melbourne all the time. So, I brushed him off. Told him to eat something greasy and that we'd be back later."

Billie turned around. "You don't have to do this."

Wyatt shook his head because even now she was giving him an out. But he was so fucking sick of hiding behind his own grief. Behind his own failings. The weight of all the secrets that he kept pressed against his chest and stole his breath.

So did the truth.

Griffin was dead.

Wyatt had to stop pretending his life was over, too. He had to step up. Make a change. Be the guy he wanted to be. Who his brother would've wanted him to be.

"He was gone by the time we got home." He blinked back tears.

Billie walked towards him. "You couldn't have known about the aneurysm. No one could have."

Deep down he did know that. Truly. The autopsy had made that much clear. Nothing could have stopped it from rupturing and taking Griffin from them all. It was the next bit that was the hardest. The bit his parents had never said to him, but he knew they'd thought it. The bit that no one in town had known until just now.

"But he didn't have to be on his own. That was my choice and I have to live with it."

His tone was gruff but the softness in Billie's eyes comforted him. Told him that she knew he was only angry with himself. No one else.

No wonder his parents couldn't find the time to answer his calls anymore.

Billie cupped his cheek. The move was so tender, so unfamiliar. He blinked away fresh tears. The irony of the moment wasn't lost on him. This was a reversal of their positions the other morning.

"It doesn't mean you have to be on your own now, though," she said.

Wyatt had hidden from this reality for so long. Refusing to acknowledge the way his soul ached for comfort and contact. Not just physical touch, although that was part of it. Anything he'd allowed himself since Griffin's death had always been transactional, accepted under the strictest of circumstances.

"Wyatt," Billie whispered.

"I don't want to be alone," he forced out, painfully aware of the weight of the gazes that were aimed at him and Billie right now.

"Come on." She slipped her hand into his. "Let's go back upstairs. Start dinner again."

7

____

This was definitely a date, and it couldn't have been more different from their first attempt, a week ago.

One, both Wyatt and Billie agreed it was actually a date. Always a good start.

Two, she was confident it wouldn't end with a heart to heart in front of all of Wattle Junction like last weekend's dinner had.

Billie tucked her singlet into the front of her shorts, so it draped nicely and grabbed her backpack. Checked she'd stowed the picnic mat properly and none of the containers she'd stacked like a food version of Tetris would spill or tip over. Through her screen door, she heard a car engine stop, a door slam shut.

Today would be different.

Better.

Billie was sure of it.

Just like she was sure it should be illegal for someone to look like Wyatt did right now. His posture was relaxed, an easy smile on his lips, hair pulled off his face in a top knot.

But the best bit? The one that made warmth spread throughout her body and settle between her legs.

He looked happy. To see her. To be here. To be himself.

It was sexy as.

Settle down, she reminded herself.

After their conversation the other night and the one that had followed upstairs on his rooftop while they ate the most delicious pasta dish, Billie had realised just how hard Wyatt was on himself. He was so used to not allowing himself to have anything nice, anything just for him. And she'd bull-dozed in there, determined to seduce him.

Seducing him was still the plan but now she could admit that her panic that their time was running out had been influenced by the other changes happening in her life. Billie might feel like she was standing in quicksand, but she couldn't just grab at the first thing for stability.

Not that there weren't parts of Wyatt she wanted to grab. Repeatedly. That went without saying.

"Good afternoon."

Butterflies filled Billie's stomach and her chest. Wyatt even sounded happy. She couldn't contain her grin. On impulse she leaned forward and kissed his cheek. His beard tickled her lips, and his skin was deliciously warm. "Hey," she said, pulling away.

Wyatt grabbed her hand and there was nothing awkward about it.

Today was going to be so, so good.

"You ready?" he asked.

With Wyatt by her side, his eyes light and her palm fitted snuggly against his? Billie was ready for anything.

～

Simple was always best. And when Wyatt groaned after biting into the miniature sponge cakes filled with strawberries and cream, Billie had to bury her smile in her glass of water. She'd made everything for their picnic from scratch. Wyatt had protested, saying he owed her a proper meal because the one last weekend had been derailed. But Billie had insisted, only just stopping herself from saying that making things for others was her love language.

Because talking about love languages? Kind of the opposite of taking things easy.

"Did you talk to your parents about the bakery?" Wyatt asked.

Billie rearranged her legs, crossing them underneath her. Wyatt's gaze dropped to her bare legs and the ache between her thighs burned a path through her stomach, landing heavily in her breasts. If he kept looking at her like that, she might forget her manners and maul him. Right here in the clearing he'd led her to. A secret little spot that deviated from one of his favourite walking tracks. The running water of the Wattle River mixed beautifully with the other sounds of nature, cocooning them in a perfect, private bubble.

"Not yet. I'm still figuring out what I want do next. If I have a proper plan, hopefully it'll soften the blow." Her cheeks heated.

"That's fair enough," Wyatt said with a faraway look in his eyes. She suspected he was thinking about his own parents and the relationship that he'd described as 'a bit distant' earlier. Billie had wanted to press. To tell him that she was sure his parents didn't blame him for not being with Griffin, but he'd changed the subject deftly, moving it to a bit of gossip about the James brothers and their auction dates. Teddy's had been spotted leaving his place the next morning, a wide smile on her face and with a slightly awkward gait.

Billie watched as Wyatt popped the last bite of his cake into his mouth, a tiny bit of cream and icing sugar clinging to his top lip.

"You've got a bit of ..." She gestured towards his mouth and Wyatt wiped the wrong side with a serviette.

"Did I get it?"

"No, it's ..." Billie leant forward and swiped the mess away, her fingers lingering on his face. They were so close. She could feel his breath on her face, the scratchiness of his beard. The thought of that against her skin and between her legs made her shiver.

"Thank you," he whispered, his words rumbling over her rapidly overheating skin.

"You're welcome." Billie was frozen in place. Letting him go was physically impossible. Not when she'd been wanting this for so long. Needing him in so many ways.

The picnic mat rustled underneath them as Wyatt scooted closer, his face pressing harder against her fingertips. Gently—reverently—he reached up to cup her face.

Is this really happening?

His gaze dropped to her mouth.

"I like you a lot, Billie," Wyatt said. Then he kissed her.

WYATT PRESSED FORWARD and twisted his hands in Billie's hair, drawing their bodies closer until they were chest-to-chest. He growled when she opened for him, sucked on his bottom lip. Everything about Billie was so delicious. Sugar lingered on her tongue and he'd bet that she'd taste sweet everywhere.

This was better than he'd imagined, and he'd pictured this moment so many times he'd lost count.

A voice in his mind whispered, "was it like this when she kissed your brother?"

He paused. It wasn't Griffin's voice that he'd been hearing. It was his own. And it needed to shut the fuck up because it was time he got out of his own way. Because it had never been like this with anyone else. And he'd forgotten two major details every time he'd agonised about what Griffin would've wanted.

What Wyatt wanted also counted.

What Billie wanted was just as important.

And she wanted him. He respected her enough to chase the taunt away as he recaptured her mouth, his hand slipping down her side, squeezing her ass.

Her past didn't matter.

His didn't, either.

All that mattered was that they were here together now. And nothing was going to ruin this moment.

When Billie pulled away, her eyes fluttered open so sweetly, Wyatt took a mental picture. A reminder that this was real. His dream girl was right in front of him, her cheeks flushed, lips swollen. Bringing her here had been a mistake because there was so much more he wanted to experience with her ... and they couldn't do that here.

Unless ... *no*. They'd agreed to take it slow. Stop putting so much pressure on themselves. Going further in a private-but-public-adjacent space seemed like an awful lot of pressure.

Didn't mean they couldn't make out, though.

"You're so beautiful," Wyatt said before dropping kisses along Billie's neck, her collarbone.

"I've wanted you to do that for so damn long." The

breathiness in her tone had him reconsidering if this little clearing, way off the hiking trail, was secluded enough for more of her kisses, more of everything.

"I wanted to. I was just all in my head."

"There's still plenty of time." Billie guided his mouth back to hers and pressed her chest against his even harder. Her nipples were hard. Maybe it was a good thing they weren't at his place. Or hers. He'd be peeling her clothes off, guiding her into his bed.

Which, again, was the opposite of taking things slow.

Wyatt breathed out carefully. Watched as her chest rose and fell, a hint of lace peeking out the top of her singlet. "I like the sound of that."

Her kisses slowed down, softening to something sweet but still addictive. His hands gripped her ass tighter. Billie tipped her head back and moaned softly. That sound was Wyatt's undoing. He lifted her and she followed his lead willingly, shifting until she was on his lap. If Wyatt slipped his hand inside her shorts, he knew he'd find her wet and wanting. His cock thickened and grew so hard it was on the precipice of becoming painful. Billie rocked against him and moaned again.

Fuck going slow.

Or waiting for the right time.

He'd waited too long already.

Wyatt slid his hands under her singlet, pushing upwards until he could cup her tits.

Jesus Christ. They were perfect handfuls. Billie shivered and started to move faster. He massaged the hard buds, dropped his head so he could suck on her neck, not caring if it left a mark. The idea of everyone knowing she was with him? He liked that. A lot.

"Oh God, Wyatt."

Goosebumps broke out across her flesh and Wyatt chased them with his tongue, burying his face in her cleavage. Fuck she smelt good here. Like strawberries and something flowery; roses, maybe. He pulled at her nipples and her hips quickened against his. "Tell me if it's too much."

"It's not enough," she whimpered setting fire to the need inside of Wyatt.

"You're so beautiful," he repeated.

She ground down against him. When one of her singlet straps slipped off her shoulder exposing delicate milky skin clad in black lace, Wyatt couldn't resist pulling the bra cup down, taking her nipple in his mouth.

Damn. Billie was sweet and *holy shit*, she felt good against his tongue, his cock. If it was this amazing while they were still mostly dressed, Wyatt couldn't think of a word to accurately describe what it would be like when they actually had sex.

Her hands found their way back into his hair and she pulled him closer. Wyatt nipped at her, and she cried out. "More. Please. Just like that."

Hold on. Could she come from this?

He had to find out.

Forgetting where they were, what his name was, why he'd taken so long to let himself have this, Wyatt yanked down the other side of Billie's top and bra. He switched to her other breast, grinning against her skin when she whimpered.

"Wyatt ..."

"Yeah, baby?"

He looked up just as her mouth formed a perfect 'o'.

"I'm going to..."

Had he thought she was beautiful before?

Because as Billie came with a throaty sigh that transformed into a strangled moan, she was magnificent. He'd bet she was a screamer in the privacy of a bedroom.

Wyatt immediately added 'make Billie scream' to his bucket list.

When she went limp, her body slumping against his, he pushed her hair off her sweaty forehead, kissed her cheek. Wyatt couldn't stop touching her. Or smiling. She might've had the orgasm, but he'd enjoyed himself just as much. Watching her lose control and let herself be free was fucking hot.

"Oh my God. I'm so embarrassed," she muttered into his chest.

"Why?"

"It's been a while. That's all."

"It was amazing. You've got nothing to be embarrassed about." Wyatt tipped her face towards his and kissed her deeply, sucking on her tongue and lips. "Don't go," he whispered when she tried to climb off his lap.

"I'm not going far." She rubbed herself against his still hard dick. "I need to repay the favour."

Wyatt captured her chin with his fingers, gazed down at her. "That's not how this works. You don't owe me anything."

"Then lie back, Wyatt, because I *want* to repay the favour."

The clouds shifted, bathing Billie in a golden glow. When he didn't move, Billie gently nudged Wyatt backwards until his shoulders rested on the picnic mat. "Billie ..."

"Wyatt." She fixed him such a supremely stern look; he couldn't help grinning. Her shirt gaped as she leaned forward, revealing the red marks his beard had left on her tits. Wyatt's smile disappeared and he was in danger of swallowing his tongue.

"I want to make you feel good. Do you have a problem with that?"

Wyatt shook his head.

"Correct answer." And then she slid down his body.

Oh, God. When a woman did that, it usually meant one thing and one thing only.

Billie undid the button at the top of his zipper.

"I've also been dreaming about this," she said, rubbing her fingertips along the hard line of his boxer-brief covered cock, her warm breath seeping through the cotton fabric.

"Lift your hips for me."

He obeyed and she pulled his cock out, her thumb swiping across the top, moistening the tip with his pre-cum. Wyatt shifted so that he was up on his elbows. No fucking way was he staring at the sky and missing the best show of his life.

Billie's tongue peeked out of her mouth and he almost came. Right then. Before she'd even tasted him. Maybe he should look back at the sky. Count some clouds. Think about what needed to be ordered for next week's service at the pub.

Warm, wet heat engulfed him as Billie took him in her mouth, sending shivers zapping around his body. *Christ.* Wyatt was going to embarrass himself. He bit his lip. Remembered the water bill was due soon.

Her hand cupped his sac and tugged as she sucked him in deeper. His breathing became choppy.

"Oh, shit," Wyatt groaned, his mind emptying of all the diversionary tactics he'd tried to employ to stop himself from coming too quickly. When his cock hit the back of her throat and Billie purred—*purred*—at Wyatt, he was a goner.

"Baby." His hand cupped her cheek, felt how full her mouth was. "I'm going to ..."

Billie sucked even harder, and Wyatt fell back onto his elbows, coming with a hoarse cry. Grabbing at Billie, he dragged her up his body, needing her close. Her strawberry scent surrounded him as he buried his head in her hair. When his breathing returned to normal, he kissed her all slow and languidly. There was no rush.

Wyatt realised with a start that it was comforting.

Natural.

"I'd say this was a pretty great first date." Even with her face pressed into his neck, Billie's words could be heard clearly.

Wyatt tipped his head back and laughed. Felt freer than he had for as long as he could remember. Billie tilted her face towards his and their gazes locked together.

"Yeah, baby. I'd say that too."

8

———

It was going to be a perfect sunset. The kind that filled the whole sky with burnt oranges, deep pinks and glowing reds before darkness swallowed them. The first wisps were chasing daylight away as Billie and Wyatt drove back into Wattle Junction.

She leaned against the head rest, let the warm breeze dance across her skin through the open window.

The song on the radio changed and Wyatt started humming.

A low pulse started in her belly because apparently, she found that sexy. There was probably nothing about Wyatt that she wouldn't find hot. Case in point: how a few kisses had turned into outdoor orgasms. Not that she regretted it. Truthfully, she was trying to figure out when they could do it—and more—again. The memory of Wyatt's touch, the power in his body, the taste of him in her mouth ... Billie squirmed in her seat.

Wyatt's quiet chuckle was like a caress.

Billie snuck a glance at him from underneath her lashes. He had one hand on the steering wheel, tapping to the beat.

His other hand sat just above her knee, flirting with the bottom of her shorts. It was official: her panties were ruined.

Billie's gaze drifted to Wyatt's shorts. Oh yeah, he was hard again. The line of his cock pressed against the zipper of his shorts. She twisted further, cast her eyes over the backseat of the 4WD.

"I know what you're thinking," he teased as they turned down High Street. They'd have to pass the pub to get to her place but if Wyatt was worried about people seeing them together like this, there was no trace of it on his face.

She met his wicked expression with an innocent one of her own. Batted her eyelashes to see if she could coax another smile out of him. He shook his head, a gentle chiding that he knew what she was doing. Billie's lips curled in response. "And what exactly is that?" she asked.

That she'd never had sex in a car? One of the best things about living in the middle of nowhere was that it was awfully easy to find quiet roads and secret spots without attracting attention.

Wyatt didn't answer, a shocked expression clouding over his face as he looked right past her. Billie twisted towards the window.

A maroon Landcruiser and off-road trailer were parked out the front of the pub. There was a whiff of familiarity about it.

Billie closed her eyes when she remembered.

They belonged to Wyatt's parents.

"Would you like to come in?" Billie asked.

It was a pointless question. She already knew the answer.

It was only a short drive but Wyatt had been different ever since he realised his parents were back. He'd been quiet and contemplative, which Billie sometimes thought was just a nicer way to describe being closed off. Just like he used to be.

"I should get back and see my parents."

She nodded. "You must have lots to catch up on."

"Hmmm." Wyatt didn't meet her gaze. He just sighed and dragged his hand through his hair. Her heart ached for him. She'd always thought he and his parents were close. That in a tragic way, Griffin's death had brought them even closer together. But after everything Wyatt had said earlier and about his guilt for not being there, she knew it wasn't so simple. Families hardly ever were. Add that she and Wyatt were now doing whatever they were doing to the already complicated Andrews' family dynamic and it might all be too much.

There'd be no more dates or kisses or the Wyatt who didn't hide away.

The man who let people see him.

Let himself have something he wanted.

Billie's stomach rolled.

Don't do it. Don't do it. Don't do— "Are you worried about what they might say?"

Wyatt's eyes snapped to hers.

"About us." It was like the words were just falling out of her mouth and she had no control over herself. "I mean, not that we've had a discussion about what this is. And we don't need to have one. Not right now. I'm sorry." She clamped her mouth shut.

Wyatt's eyes softened and Billie breathed out slowly when he reached for her hands, pressing their palms together and linking their fingers. His touch was soft and gentle. Despite the heat that lingered from the summer's day, Billie shivered.

"We're an us," Wyatt said. His words were firm and strong—exactly the reassurance Billie had needed.

"We are?" She bit her lip and tried to tamp down the joy that unfurled in her chest, spread throughout her limbs.

Wyatt tilted his head, a wry smile transforming his face. "You think I do that with just anyone?"

Heat flooded her cheeks. "No. I just ..." She took a deep breath. "I was panicking that this might be over before it really got started." Ducking her chin, Billie studied the wooden planks that made up the small verandah at the front of her little cottage. The white paint was chipped. It was another thing that needed a refresher around here.

She looked up when Wyatt said her name.

"My parents will probably have an opinion about us. Hell, the whole town will. But I don't think it will be bad."

"Do you want me to come with you?" Because she would. Billie would go to the ends of the Earth with this man if it meant they could be together.

Wyatt brushed his lips across hers like this kind of familiar kiss had always bookended their days.

Like they really were an us.

And his parents' opinion mattered but it wouldn't define them.

Nobody's would.

WYATT'S PARENTS were sitting at the kitchen counter like they owned the place.

And yeah, technically, they did.

"Wyatt!" His mother, Jennie, rushed forward, arms outstretched. "How are you?"

He smiled tightly and returned her hug. She was smaller than he remembered but her perfume was the same. Lavender and mint. "Good. You?"

"I can't tell you how much I've been looking forward to a real bath."

"Looks like the upgrades are all finished." His father, Peter, was all business as he stood. No hello. Or hug. Wyatt would've settled for a handshake, but it wasn't offered.

"I wasn't expecting you guys." He congratulated himself for keeping his tone polite. Bland. There was no hint of the hurt thrumming through Wyatt's veins. He'd spoken to them six weeks ago and they were in Western Australia. Up near Broome. Almost as far away from Wattle Junction as possible. Neither had mentioned their plan to return.

Peter shrugged. "Decided it was time to come back."

"I've been trying to call you."

"You know the reception's rubbish."

Wyatt shoved his hands in his pockets. "Are you planning on hanging around?"

"Why? You trying to get rid of us already?" Peter played it off as a joke but there was a hard edge to his words.

"Just asking, Dad."

"We're still deciding." Jennie looped her arm through his and dragged him over to the couch. "Now, come. Tell me everything. I heard Owen James is moving back here. Never thought I'd see the day he chose Wattle Junction over the city. He's always been my least favourite of all those boys."

Wyatt bristled. Owen was a good guy. He could be stand-offish with strangers but like the whole James family, his heart was in the right place, and he was always ready to help anyone. "He's bought the old law office. Teddy says he'll be starting his own firm."

"Lulu must be thrilled to have all her boys back home."

Previously, Wyatt would have been wounded by the hidden meaning in his mother's statement. Because it wasn't hard to crack that code. Jennie would never have both her boys back home.

Probably, he should be sympathetic.

But Wyatt wasn't in the mood. He pushed to his feet.

"What's going on?" he asked.

"What do you mean?" Peter said.

"You show up without warning—"

"—I didn't realise we needed an invitation to come back to our home!" Peter raised his eyebrows in challenge.

"That's not what I meant. You're both always welcome here. Of course, you are. But I don't understand why you didn't tell me. Or answer any of my calls over the last few weeks."

His father waved a dismissive hand. "We were out of range a lot."

"I sent you other messages, too." Peter and Jennie had a special two-way satellite messenger that always had coverage, regardless of where they were in Australia.

"We thought you'd like the surprise," Jennie said quietly but Wyatt didn't believe her. Anything with mystery or hidden intrigue had always, *always* been Griffin's wheelhouse. And if they wanted to surprise Wyatt, why did they park their enormous camper out the front of the pub? The thing was roughly the same size as a billboard.

Really, they hadn't even thought about Wyatt.

He gritted his teeth.

"I think I'm going to run that bath." Jennie patted her thighs and stood.

"Good idea. I'm going to get ready for bed. Was an early start," Peter said.

Wyatt glanced at the clock. It was just after eight. They hadn't seen each other for three and a half years and they couldn't even pretend to care about what was going on in his life. Or the pub. He'd hurt them more than he'd realised and as a sharp pain seared his chest, he knew they'd hurt him, too. Really hurt him. And they didn't care.

He picked up his keys. "I'm heading out," he said.

"What?" Jennie said.

"I'll see you in the morning. And we can run through everything with the pub."

"Where are you going?" Peter asked like Wyatt was fourteen again.

"I'll be back in time to open up."

Just like he had been ever since they'd left.

ALL THE THOUGHTS that had plagued Wyatt on the walk to Billie's house disappeared when she opened her front door in a tiny light blue robe with wet hair.

Thank God he hadn't holed up in his room, or gone to Teddy's or Nate's.

"Hi," Billie said uncertainly, one hand wrapped around the door jamb.

"Hey."

"You okay?"

Wyatt was now. "Yep. I just needed"—to not be trapped in the past—"some fresh air."

Billie looked over his shoulder. Her street was quiet aside from the sound of a few sprinklers *tick-tick-ticking* as streams of water arced over thirsty lawns. "Do you want to come in? I was just watching some TV." She fiddled with the tie on her robe. It clung to her small frame, curving around her breasts, cinching in tight around her waist.

She was so perfect. Now that Wyatt was allowing himself to think about how much he wanted her, drooling was going to be a problem. His gaze dipped to her bare legs, the sunshine-y yellow nail polish on her toenails.

Because that's what she was. Billie was sunshine and warmth and everything good in this world. Fuck he was lucky that she wanted him. He didn't deserve her patience but he'd be grateful for it, forever.

She shifted her weight from one foot to the other.

"Wyatt?" Doubt weighed down his name.

Oh, shit. Did Billie think he was here just because of what they'd done earlier? Why hadn't Wyatt stopped to consider that? Because all he'd been able to think about was getting away from his parents and the only place he'd wanted to be was here with Billie.

"I'm sorry," he said.

Billie's brows pinched together.

"I should have called or something. I didn't mean to ... I just had to get away. I'm not here for sex." Wyatt groaned. What a time to be terrible with words. He'd have to try harder because Billie deserved so much more. "I want more than that with you. I just wanted to see you."

A slow smile spread across Billie's face. "Fancy some dessert?" She hitched her thumb over her shoulder, presumably towards where her kitchen was.

"Dessert sounds great. What are you watching?" Wyatt asked.

She winced, flushing adorably. "Just some reality TV. Have you ever heard of *Take a Chance on Love*?"

Wyatt shook his head. Hang on. Maybe he'd seen an ad for it? Where people married strangers, or something?

"Then you are in for a treat. It's the perfect distraction from reality."

He nodded and Billie grabbed his arm and dragged him inside. He clocked the buttery yellow walls with white skirting boards and cornices. Let himself be pushed down on the soft grey couch covered in way too many cushions.

"Wait here," she said.

Billie's footsteps disappeared down the hall to his right and Wyatt sank back further into the couch. Photo frames were scattered around the television and there were a lot of plants. It was cosy and homey. He'd bet it was Billie's favourite room in the mornings when sunlight streamed through the large windows. He could picture her in the armchair, a book on her lap and cup of coffee curled in her hand.

Wyatt blinked.

He could see himself there, too. Billie on his lap, his chin on her shoulder, sitting quietly. Not needing to talk to fill the silence but content to just be together.

He was in so deep with her. The thought should've scared him, especially since everything between them was still brand new and he didn't know what his parents would say. How they'd feel about it all.

"Okay." Billie walked into the room with a tray. "I've got ice cream and the very last sponge cake. Someone was hungry this afternoon." She winked at Wyatt and he realised, he really didn't care what anyone else thought.

Billie placed the tray on the coffee table before sitting down next to him and leaning against his side. Strawberry surrounded him.

"Let me catch you up," Billie said, slipping her arm

through Wyatt's. "That's Alice. She married Phoenix on the first season. He's a musician and whatever. Everyone loves them. They have the perfect marriage, blah, blah, blah."

Billie kept talking, her voice low and soothing.

This was it, Wyatt realised. This was the future that he wanted. Here with Billie all curled up on the couch. Her shampoo tickling his nose. The weight of her body against his. A real partnership that would grow and change and be the best constant in his life.

And he'd do whatever it took to protect what they had.

9

A shrill sound woke Billie and she blinked.

"That's me," Wyatt mumbled next to her, blessedly silencing his alarm. "Sorry."

His arms wrapped around her and Billie curled back into his body. Last night came back in a flood of memories: hours on the couch, snuggled up and discovering Wyatt was the perfect binge-watching partner. He didn't fuss with his phone or pretend to watch. He'd been fully engaged, asking questions about what had happened in previous episodes, why anyone would voluntarily sign up to marry someone they'd never met before. He'd laughed so hard when Billie described a fight between two of the women over who ate the last of the sushi because it was a metaphor for something she couldn't remember now because her mind was still waking up. The last thing she remembered was falling asleep on the couch with him.

She squeezed her eyes shut and savoured how right it felt to start the day in Wyatt's arms.

Because, seriously, how lucky was Billie? The only thing

better than waking up with Wyatt? Getting to do it twice in one night.

She pushed back with her hips, eyes flying open, when Wyatt ground his hard cock against her.

Hopefully, Billie was about to get even luckier.

Wyatt's hands gripped her waist, a soft curse falling from his lips.

"Do you have to go?" she whispered.

Please say no. The sun was barely even awake and it was her morning off. She groaned softly, remembering Wyatt had mentioned he was on the opening shift today.

"That's my running alarm. I don't start for another two hours."

Billie twisted around, her foot coasting along the length of his calf. "Which means ..."

Wyatt pulled her closer until their bodies were pressed against each other. "I don't have to go, unless you want me to."

She absolutely did not want that. She'd tie him up to stop him from leaving if she had to. A wave of arousal rolled through Billie at the thought of Wyatt with his hands bound, totally at her mercy. Another time, *definitely.*

"I'll be right back," she whispered, ducking into the tiny ensuite off her bedroom. When she returned, Wyatt was sitting up in her bed. Shirtless ... and woah. The man was pure muscle. God bless all those kegs he had to move around. His dedication to the gym and running with the rest of the football team. Billie was going to trace the outline of his abs with her tongue. Tease the flat brown nipples that shouldn't have called to her as much as they did but if she didn't get her mouth on them ASAP, and hear more of those little noises that he made when she tasted his golden skin,

Billie was going to lose her mind. The waistband of his boxers peeked out above the sheet pooled around his hips.

"You look good in my bed," she said when he looked up and caught her staring.

Wyatt's eyes darkened, lingering on where her hard nipples strained against the oversize t-shirt she wore to bed. It was the opposite of sexy. Literally plain white, with a stretched-out neckline and so baggy it was approaching sack territory but something—okay, *fine*, the large bulge in the sheet across Wyatt's lap—told her he didn't care.

"You look good in everything," he replied with a mischievous grin.

"You think so, huh?"

He crooked a finger at her. "Come here and I'll show how good I think you look, after I've brushed my teeth."

Billie didn't need to be asked twice. "Don't brush your teeth." No way was she letting him out of her bed right now.

Wyatt rose up on to his knees, the sheet falling to the bed. His cock was huge. Bigger than it had felt in her mouth and her hands—which was really saying something because it had been deliciously big. Like it'd be the best kind of stretch imaginable. Wyatt pulled her into a kiss that sent fireworks fizzing through her body.

"Are you sure?" he asked when he pulled away.

Billie's head was spinning. She grabbed Wyatt's shoulders for support, her hand resting on his largest tattoo. He'd gotten the griffin after his brother had passed away, adding more pieces quickly until he almost had a full sleeve. She added his tattoos to the list of things she wanted to lick.

"So sure." Billie fused their mouths together and straddled him. His cock pressed up against her sending a fresh wave of slickness to the aching place between her legs.

Wyatt pulled away and lifted the bottom of her shirt.

"Can I take this off?" His hands skated up along her ribs and Billie shivered, suddenly shy. Which was silly. He'd seen her topless just yesterday. Made her come and she'd done the same to him. But this was different. There'd be no going back after this. If he changed his mind, she didn't know if she'd recover.

Then she remembered what he'd said when he arrived on her doorstep, his eyes heavy with disappointment and a fog of sadness lingering around him. Wyatt wanted more than sex with her.

They were an us.

She had to trust him.

"Ready, baby?"

Billie raised her arms, her nipples tightening even more when the cool air of her bedroom hit them. Wyatt leaned forward, started sucking, stoking the fire within her to an inferno in seconds. "I fucking love your tits," he growled and Billie cried out, reaching for his boxers. Why was he still wearing them?

"Do you have a condom?"

Billie didn't look away from him. "In the bedside drawer." She was lost in the majesty that was Wyatt in her bed, hair all messy and eyes all dark with desire. Her gaze burnt a path down his well-defined chest and stacked abs to the thick dick she couldn't wait to slide down on.

Wyatt shifted underneath her, pressing up and Billie groaned. "Get these off."

She scooted to the side, tossing her drenched panties to the floor. As soon as Wyatt had freed his cock, Billie was on her knees, licking the thick tip, playing with his balls, chasing those little sounds.

He tapped her on the ass. "Bring that pretty pussy up here."

The mouth on him. So unlike any of her previous lovers. Billie's eyes flared as he repositioned her until his beard was tickling the soft skin of her thighs. She groaned around his cock when he pushed one finger and then another inside her.

"So fucking wet," he murmured before biting her leg lightly.

She shuddered. Oh God. There was no gentle preamble, no tender swipe of his tongue. Wyatt just dove right in, sucked on her clit like his life depended on it.

This was how Billie was going to die and she wasn't mad about it. Wrenching her mouth from Wyatt's cock, she breathed in choppily, sucking oxygen down into her lungs.

"Thank God," he said, flipping her on to her back. "I was so close. Too close."

"Yeah?" Happiness curled through Billie but Wyatt distracted her by picking up the condom. The muscles in his arms flexed as he rolled it on.

"Scoot down, baby," he said. "Don't want you to bang your head."

It was official. Wyatt Andrews was everything. He was darkness and light, all sharp edges and tenderness, more perfect than she'd ever imagined.

Billie spread her legs and pulled him down on top of her. Wyatt closed his eyes when he pushed inside her, stretching her. His breath was a hard pant across Billie's face and she grabbed his shoulders again.

"Billie. Fuck, you're tight."

She tilted her hips, hooking her ankles around his waist. "Give me more," she whispered. "I can take it."

Wyatt's eyes flew open and Billie pushed up to meet him. She'd never been so full.

"Change of plans," he said, pulling back into shallow,

teasing thrusts. "We're calling in sick. Not leaving the bed today."

Billie was about to reply when Wyatt surprised her, snapping his hips forward. And *ohhhh*, pleasure climbed up her spine, making it hard to speak or even breathe. She arched her back and twined her fingers through his hair. Like a magnetic force was pulling him, Wyatt dropped his head to her chest and sucked on her nipple. The scratch of his beard made Billie shiver.

They moved together like they'd done this a million times before and Billie smothered a whimper as her pleasure built.

"I want to hear you." Wyatt pushed her higher, driving into her at a gruelling pace. His hand found Billie's clit and she exploded, screaming his name.

His rhythm changed and Wyatt lifted his head. Met her gaze. Came with the same hoarse cry that had filled her dreams.

He was beautiful.

"We could've been doing that this whole time?" he mumbled into the side of her breast. "I'm an idiot."

Billie breathed out a quiet laugh, still deep in her post orgasm bliss. "*I'm* an idiot," she repeated.

She pushed Wyatt's hair off his face. He was relaxed and happy. No hint of regret.

This was going to be great.

~

"Your brother's ex-girlfriend, really?" Peter said as soon as Wyatt pushed through the front door. Damn it. Wyatt had meant what he said to Billie. Hiding from all their responsibilities and staying in bed would've been a much better way to spend the day. But she'd smiled softly and told him to go to work. Tell his parents before someone else did. Looked like that ship had sailed.

"We can talk about this later. I've got to get downstairs. Just need a fresh work shirt. Where's Mum?"

His father didn't budge from the hallway. "Still sleeping. What about Griffin?"

Wyatt bristled. He wasn't going to let his parents take away his happiness. Not anymore, starting right now. "What about him, Dad?"

"I imagine he'd have something to say about this."

Griffin would've. Where Wyatt was more reserved and kept his cards close to his chest, Griffin had never met anyone he couldn't talk to. It was part of why everyone loved him – and why his loss had left such a huge hole in their family. Wyatt hadn't realised until it was too late that Griffin had literally been the glue holding them all together.

"I think he'd be happy for us."

Peter's snort made Wyatt's shoulders tense but he ignored the bait, digging through his drawer until he found a Wattle Junction Hotel shirt. He'd find a way to be the bigger person and still stand his ground. Try to salvage his relationship with his parents. "Let's have dinner tonight. I'll bring up your favourites and we can catch up properly. Talk about the pub and what you and Mum have got planned."

Like were they back for good?

"He was going to ask Billie for another chance."

Wyatt tugged his shirt over his head. "But he didn't. And she would've said no."

"Still ..." Peter frowned at the ground.

"Still what? Billie's not a thing. She didn't belong to him. And she doesn't belong to me. She's her own person and she gets to make her own choices. Like everyone else, including me."

"And she's your choice?"

Wyatt didn't hesitate. "Yes."

Peter nodded and deflated. A heaviness settled in Wyatt's chest as a faraway look filled his father's eyes. "I still can't believe he's gone."

Wyatt exhaled slowly. "I know, Dad. But letting our lives move forward doesn't mean we're going to forget him. Griffin will always be a part of us. We'll talk more tonight, okay?"

WYATT WAS behind the bar when Billie walked in. And that easy smile on her face? He'd like to think he put it there.

"Never thought I'd see the day," Teddy teased as he skirted around Wyatt to reach for a new bottle of chardonnay for Lulu and Joan to share with their book club. The women were all sitting around three tables holding what Wyatt guessed were romances based on the shirtless man on the covers. He wished his mother would join them, even if his dad would scoff about their reading choices.

"Shut up," Wyatt said, unable to keep the laugh out of his voice.

"Hi," Billie said shyly, her cheeks flushed.

Even though they hadn't discussed how they planned to act in public, because Lord knew people were going to have opinions, Wyatt didn't hesitate. He leaned over the bar, quirked an eyebrow at Billie and said, "C'mere, baby."

"Really?"

"Yep." He let the 'p' pop, hoping she'd blush again. Later he'd kiss every place that blush stained her body.

"Everyone's watching," Billie whispered. She licked her lips as she rested her forearms on the bar. Mirth danced in her eyes.

"So?" Wyatt lowered his voice. "I want to say hello to my girl."

Apparently, he hadn't lowered his voice enough because Teddy hooted and a chorus of "awwwws" erupted from Lulu's table. No wonder the James brothers always referred to them as the Old Girls' Gossip Brigade. They clearly had Vulcan hearing.

But Wyatt didn't care. He wasn't about to miss out on any of Billie's kisses. The sooner everyone got used to the idea that they were together, the better. And his parents hadn't ventured into the pub at all, so it wasn't like they were rubbing their noses in it.

Billie rolled her eyes and Wyatt took that as his cue, pressing forward and placing a soft kiss against her mouth. "Hi," he said when they broke apart, pleased to see her lips curved in a dreamy smile. Probably his were doing the same. Subtly, Wyatt checked his watch. Maybe he could convince her to join him on his lunch break.

"When did all this happen?" Joan called out.

"Hmmm?" Wyatt said, all casual nonchalance. It was like putting on an old jacket. It felt familiar but not quite right. New goal: be more like old Wyatt, the guy he'd been before Griffin died.

"Don't play coy with me!" Joan teased. "It was the auction, wasn't it?"

Billie laughed and the sound lit Wyatt up on the inside. "Maybe?" He shrugged.

"Well, I like it," Lulu said.

"Me too," Joan added.

It was a small thing, really, but knowing they had a few

people on their side made everything easier. Dinner would still be a challenge, though.

"How are your parents?" Billie asked softly when the meals for Lulu and her friends started coming out.

"They're ..." Wyatt considered his words carefully.

"Upset?"

He squeezed her hand. "Surprised. You know how they are. What did yours say?"

Billie groaned softly. "They're very excited. They want you to come over soon. I think they love you more than they love me. There was gushing, Wyatt. My mum said you're a catch."

"Damn right he is." Teddy slapped Wyatt on the shoulder as he passed him.

"Anyway, I better go. I just wanted to make sure you were okay."

Wyatt picked up a tea towel and started drying the rack of glasses Teddy had just brought back. "I'm great. Everything's going to be fine."

And it would be. Eventually. Once his parents got used to the idea of him and Billie being a couple.

Right?

10

———

"The books look good." Jennie cut into her steak. The citronella from the candles mixed with the sweet scent of the roses that Wyatt's mother had spent the day tending to.

"The accommodation's very popular. Everyone's still talking about the themed rooms you designed." It wasn't a lie. Anyone who stayed at the pub commented on the different design styles Wyatt's mother had chosen. By far the most popular one was the Australiana room with its gumtree wallpaper and bird shaped light fittings.

"I'm so glad." Jennie smiled. The setting sun behind her painted the sky a myriad different colours. "You've done a great job here, Wyatt. Keeping everything running."

Always uncomfortable with compliments, Wyatt pushed a forkful of coleslaw around his plate. "Where was your favourite place to visit?" he asked Peter, trying to draw him into the conversation.

"We want to sell the pub," his father said.

"Peter!" Jennie hissed, shaking her head.

"What? It's true. We want to sell the pub."

Déjà vu washed over Wyatt as he remembered Billie telling him about having a similar conversation with her parents.

"You're not planning on staying in Wattle Junction?" The pang of sadness Wyatt expected didn't come.

"Actually, we thought we might move to the beach. Find a nice little shack somewhere close to the water. I want to be able to hear the waves," Jennie said.

It did sound nice but the nearest beach was hours away.

"It's really that bad? Being here?" Wyatt asked quietly, unable to look at his parents. He didn't need to see the sadness in their eyes. He knew it was there.

"He's everywhere," Jennie whispered. "That's why we can't stay. Not full-time. We'll still come and visit, and you can do the same."

Funny. Not funny ha ha, obviously, but funny interesting. His memories of Griffin here were exactly why Wyatt couldn't leave.

"I understand." And he did, actually. Finally, in this awkwardly stilted conversation, it all made sense. None of them could keep living in the past. People grieved in different ways and on different timelines. The idea of living somewhere that didn't have memories of Griffin embedded in every inch of the place made Wyatt's chest pull tight. For him, the echoes of Griffin scattered through Wattle Junction were a comfort. But for his parents, they were too much.

And that was okay.

It didn't mean they loved Griffin more. Or didn't care about what Wyatt was doing.

Probably his relationship with them would improve once they were settled somewhere that brought them peace.

Wyatt had been so busy living half a life trying to keep everything together, that he hadn't realised his parents were doing the same thing. If leaving Wattle Junction was what they needed to do, then that was what was best for them.

"You don't ever think about leaving?" Jennie dabbed at her eyes. "If I had one regret, it would be that we left you here. Trapped you, really."

The rooftop provided a bird's eye view of Wattle Junction. To his left, Wyatt could see Teddy's ute parked outside Owen's new office. The brothers were carrying paint and other tools into the building. Maybe later, he'd stop by and ask if they needed any help. He twisted his head in the other direction, watching a group of older kids kick a soccer ball around the big park opposite the pub.

Wattle Junction had always been his home and it always would be.

"I know it's different for you," he said, "but there's nowhere else I'd rather be."

"Because of Billie," Peter said quietly. There was no trace of his father's anger from this morning. Just the quiet sadness that had lingered in his voice ever since Griffin passed.

"Not just Billie, but she is a part of it."

"I'm not surprised," Jennie said. "She's watched you for many years. And I've seen the way you look at her. I think it's a good thing."

Wyatt shot his mother a grateful smile. "It *is* a good thing. The best thing, actually. And I know it's awkward but if you give us a chance, I'm sure you'll see how great it is."

"We can try. Can't we, Peter? It's what Griffin would've wanted. For Wyatt to be happy."

Calm settled over Wyatt's skin. So often he got lost in

thinking about what Griffin had missed out on that he forgot the most important thing. Griffin had loved Wyatt. He'd been a great brother. He would've supported anything that made Wyatt happy. Just like Wyatt had always done the same for him.

"There's one more thing." Wyatt waited until they were both looking at him. "I'd like to buy the pub from you."

It had been a part of the fabric of their lives for so long, and while it was in his parents' past, it was destined to be Wyatt's future.

Just like the woman he'd secretly loved for so long.

"I heard a rumour ..."

Billie stopped arranging the pies she'd just taken out of the oven into their display case.

"Mum," she sighed. "We're still together. No, we're not engaged. No, we haven't discussed that. It's still new."

Daphne scoffed. "You and Wyatt were always destined to end up together. But that wasn't what I was talking about. Why didn't you mention that Max had stopped by?"

Because I've been too busy spending my nights wrapped around Wyatt or trying to get the courage together to tell you about my grand new plan?

"He's getting married. He wanted to give me a heads up," Billie said. "And he wants me to make their wedding cake. You know how much I like making cakes."

Daphne nodded absentmindedly and started wiping down the serving counter. "I'm sure you'll do a wonderful job."

Billie placed the tongs back on the hook at the side of

the pie case. The bakery was empty. It was just her and her parents. She remembered the hushed conversation she and Wyatt had shared last night after he finished dinner with his parents. How sweetly he'd smiled when he told her that he'd made it clear that he was serious about her. Wyatt hadn't hesitated to go to bat for their relationship, stressing how happy it made him. It was time for her to do the same. Be honest about what she wanted. "Actually, there was something I wanted to talk to you both about."

"Is this a flip the sign conversation?" Daphne asked.

"Looks like one to me." Ben winked. He locked the door and twisted the sign, so it said 'back in five minutes'.

"I don't want to take over the bakery." Okay. Billie was going with the band-aid approach to delivering her decision. Would've been helpful to know in advance but whatever. "I love working here with you guys. I really do. And I'm excited for you to retire and do whatever it is that you want to do."

"But you want to make cakes and desserts?" Daphne guessed.

Billie should've known her mother would see what had been right in front of her for the last few weeks. "They've always been my favourites."

"Darling, you know we think your cakes are amazing but the demand for specialty cakes out here isn't all that high."

"Which is why I'd like to stay on here part-time while the new owner is settling in. I'll use that time to get my business established. Hopefully some of the local cafes and restaurants will be interested in stocking my desserts."

Ben knocked his shoulder against Billie's. "Something tells me the hotel will put in a large order."

"Probably." Billie's lips curled into a soft smile, and she

didn't miss the way her parents noticed, their own grins appearing, too.

"All we want is for you to be happy. This is what's going to make you happy?" Daphne asked.

"It will."

"Then we're all for it. We'll start looking for a buyer."

"But while we're still the bosses, why don't you take off? Go find that man of yours?"

Her parents were the actual best. Billie untied her apron and gave them both a kiss on the cheek.

BILLIE FOUND Wyatt in his office, squinting at the computer in front of him. His parents were sitting next to him.

"Hey," she said when they all looked up. He resembled them both in different ways. He had the same nose, same strong jaw line as his father. But his eyes? They were Jennie's.

"Hey, baby," Wyatt said.

Peter shook his head at the term of endearment and panic rose inside Billie's chest. She'd seen them a few times in passing since they'd been home and it had been fine. Stilted and awkward but each time it got easier. Her worry receded a second later when Peter elbowed Jennie, the ghost of a smile on his face. That smile was all Griffin's.

"I didn't mean to interrupt. We can catch up later."

"It's okay. I think we're done here." Peter stood and gathered a few papers together.

"Maybe we could do dinner soon, Billie," Jennie said shyly and Billie recognised the moment for what it was. An olive branch.

"I'd like that," she said.

"Wyatt can fill us in on the details later." They left the office, pulling the door closed behind them.

"Things seem better?" Billie perched on the edge of Wyatt's desk, loving the way his hand settled on her thigh immediately. Like he couldn't be near her and not touch her. She felt the same way.

"My parents are moving to the beach."

"How do you feel about that?"

"Pretty good." Wyatt scooted his chair back, making space for her to shuffle along the desk until she was right in front of him. "They're going to sell the pub to me."

"Wyatt! That's amazing!"

"I know we haven't been together all that long, but ..."

Billie couldn't stop her biggest grin from breaking free. Was a conversation like this really too early when they'd been doing this dance for years? Sometimes time was nothing but a relative concept.

"... I don't want to make any big life decisions without discussing them with you. Because something that affects my future, affects yours." He nudged her legs apart, standing and moving into the space between them. Billie tilted her head back so she could see his eyes properly. They were clear and bright and this ... was her future. Right in front of her.

"I think you should buy the pub." Billie's hands gripped his hips and pulled him closer.

"Yeah?"

"Yep." Her hands slipped around to his firm ass. His cock pressed against her thigh. "And you should put in a standing order for desserts from my new business."

"Done. I'll take one of everything."

"Shall we seal our deal with a handshake?" Billie teased.

He moved his hips and Billie tipped her head back.

"I've got a better idea. Don't move," Wyatt whispered into her ear.

Once the door was locked, Wyatt was back, all hungry eyes and hands. "Here?" she grinned as he peppered kisses down her neck, pushing the thin straps of her dress off her shoulders.

"If you're game."

"With you? I'm game for all of it." Billie guided his mouth up to hers, pulling him into a deep kiss. Something fell off the desk, hitting the ground with a smash but Wyatt's gaze never left hers.

He brushed her hair off her face. "I'm in love with you, Billie."

His heartbeat was steady under her fingertips. "I think I've been in love with you for a long time. But this? Being with you now? And really knowing you? It's better than I could have ever imagined."

"So much better," Wyatt whispered. "Got to have you now."

Billie reached for his jeans. "Then take me."

LATER, after Billie had splashed water on her face and finger-combed her hair, she joined Wyatt in the dining room. He was behind the bar, his biceps flexing and a wide smile on his face. He grabbed her before she could sit down and brushed his lips across hers. The casually possessive move, coupled with what they'd just done in his office, made her heart burst.

A confident smile blossomed on his face and flutters broke out in her stomach and her chest, as she settled herself on a stool across from him. Wyatt was about to ask her what had always been—and always would be—her favourite question.

"What'll it be, baby?"

THE END.

EPILOGUE

(one year later)

If Wyatt had his way, they'd still be in bed. And he and Billie definitely wouldn't have an audience.

"You okay?" Billie's hand slipped inside his. Her touch grounded him, reminded him that he wasn't alone.

Wyatt blinked and looked out across the wide clearing. Wattle Junction was in the distance, his pub standing tall and proud like a sentinel. Still, bringing his friends to such a private place wasn't easy, even if they were doing him a massive favour. The James brothers all trailed past, their arms full of building supplies. As if they sensed Wyatt and Billie needed a minute they didn't stop, their voices low and steps as quiet as possible.

"I'm more worried about you. Are you sure it's not too hot?" Wyatt twisted so Billie was in his arms, her back pressed against his chest. His hands ghosted over the barely there bump that they were still keeping a secret.

It was easily the best secret Wyatt had ever had. And sharing it with Billie? Knowing their baby would be here in five-ish months? Talk about a dream come true.

"I'm fine. The fresh air is helping."

Wyatt sighed. There'd been plenty of fresh air flowing through their little cottage this morning, the windows thrown open so they could hear the birds. But it hadn't stopped Billie from losing her breakfast.

"Maybe you should sit down?" Worry for Billie and their unborn child crept across Wyatt's skin and he cursed himself again for agreeing to let her come on this hike. She'd been so tired lately.

"Somewhere to sit would be nice." Billie shifted so they were face to face. "Best go help the others build that bench, huh?"

Wyatt rolled his eyes but couldn't stop his lips from tugging into a small smile. "At least stay in the shade and have a drink. Maybe some crackers?" He'd made sure to pack two boxes of her favourites.

"Yes, boss." Billie winked and Wyatt shook his head, trying to tamp down the wide grin that threatened to break free. Ever since she'd started working at the Wattle Junction Hotel as the new dessert chef in addition to her fledgling cake business, Billie had insisted on calling him boss in private. Always with a teasing lilt in her voice and a sparkle in her eye. He was pretty sure that their little secret had been created the first time she'd done it.

He waited until she'd found a comfortable spot underneath a wattle tree. Then he headed over to where his friends were. Owen was holding the instructions while Nate and Rafferty arranged all the pieces of timber. Teddy was shirtless because ... well, Teddy never needed a reason to get his top off.

"Time to build," Owen said, and handed Wyatt a drill.

THIS HAD DEFINITELY BEEN one of Billie's better ideas even if her hips were killing her and she would have loved a nap. The first trimester had kicked her butt and so far, the second one wasn't much better.

"All done?" she asked, pushing to her feet when the guys started packing away all their tools. She moved over to where Wyatt was standing next to a forest green bench bolted to one of the large flat rocks at the back of the clearing. No one had objected when Wyatt asked the council for special permission to build the bench himself. But he'd surprised her by accepting the James brothers' offer to help. Just thinking about how Wyatt had become more and more like his old self over the past year made Billie emotional. It was why she'd insisted on coming along today, too.

"Just got the plaque to go." Wyatt pulled her into his arms and Billie breathed in the hint of sweat that lingered on his skin. It mixed with the eucalyptus and earthy scent that filled the air around them.

"Speaking of that," Owen interrupted their cuddle and she realised all the brothers had their backpacks on. "We'll get out of your hair. Let you guys have some privacy."

Gratitude flowed through Billie's tired body. The James brothers truly deserved every bit of adoration that was thrown their way.

"Thanks again," Wyatt said and Billie echoed his words.

She waited until they were alone to speak. "It looks good." Billie nodded towards the bench. "Griffin would've liked it."

"He always said that somewhere comfortable to sit was all this place needed."

Billie reached into the backpack Wyatt had insisted on carrying for her and pulled out the small plaque they'd had made. Griffin's name was written in a simple font, below the words 'in memory of'. She squeezed Wyatt's hand as she passed it to him. He lifted the drill and twenty seconds later it was in place, the mid-morning sun glinting off the metal.

Wyatt's heavy sigh wrapped around her and this time, she pulled him into her arms. There was nothing Billie could do to take away his pain so she did what she always did. She held his hand, brushed the loose tendrils of hair that had escaped his man bun off his face and stood with him in his grief. In a different universe, Griffin would've been the first person they told their news too. A part of her wondered if that's why Wyatt had wanted to keep their baby news a secret for so long. Just until he could have a moment with his brother's memory in his favourite place.

Billie waited, giving Wyatt the time he needed. His heartbeat was steady under her fingertips and over the top of his shirt, Billie traced the place where her name was tattooed over his heart.

Wyatt's big palm slipped down her front and settled against her stomach. "He'd have been a great uncle."

Her smile was automatic. "He would've."

Wyatt guided her over to the new bench and pulled her onto his lap. Would he still be able to do this when her belly was so big she couldn't see her toes?

"When we get back into town, let's go see your parents. Tell them about the baby," Wyatt said.

"Yeah?" She tipped her chin down to look into his eyes.

"Yeah. We can tell mine on the weekend when we visit

them. It's time." Wyatt smiled, squeezing her thigh. "Should probably tell them about the wedding as well."

Billie shimmied a little on his lap, clapping her hands. Wyatt's soft chuckle fizzed through her body, like there were sparklers inside her veins. "I'm so lucky. I can't wait to marry you and have your baby."

"I'm the lucky one," Wyatt said and brushed his nose against hers. Billie's breath caught in her throat. To think they'd almost missed out on this amazing life together.

"But are you sure you don't want something fancier?" Wyatt's brows were furrowed. This wasn't the first time he'd asked her this.

"A sunset ceremony with a few friends and family in the roof top garden of the pub is perfect. I just need you. Nothing else."

Love blazed out of Wyatt's eyes and Billie basked in it. Hoped he saw the same thing when he looked at her. This love was the best thing that had ever happened to her. She linked her arms around Wyatt's neck and leant in until their lips were almost touching.

"I love you, Billie." His words caressed her skin.

"I love you, too."

KEEP READING FOR A SNEAK PEEK AT THE REALITY OF US, BOOK 1 IN THE WATTLE JUNCTION SERIES.

THE REALITY OF US

(A SNEAK PEEK)

1
———————

The warning lights on the dash blurred as Alice blinked, her newly ringless left hand swiping at the tears threatening to spill. She sucked in a few deep breaths. Crying wouldn't achieve anything other than ruining her smoky eye make-up. And today *wasn't* the day to try and make the sad clown look popular.

Alice fiddled with the radio, desperate to find a pounding beat to drown out her thoughts, but the plastic knob snapped off. Heavy static saturated the air like humidity right before a summer storm. She tossed the broken piece into the backseat, where the remnants of her old life swallowed it whole. Half her wardrobe was shoved into suitcases and bin bags in the back of the old Volvo AWD she'd inherited from her grandfather.

Alice drove on, the white noise somehow magically speeding up to mimic the way her heart rate increased every time she glanced at Google Maps. Not because she was worried about getting lost on a straight road with no traffic, which, *okay, fine,* had happened before, but rather because of the banner notifications rolling across the top of the screen. The avalanche of missed calls, text messages and social media alerts made her empty stomach roll. Two years ago, this would've filled her with joy. Now she just wanted to hide.

Her mother's piercing gaze flashed up on the screen—again—but she let the call ring out. What was the point in answering when she knew how the conversation would go? Marguerite Aspinall would demand Alice return to Melbourne and follow whatever plan her parents had decided on, like they always did when she messed up. Then Alice would lash out and say something she'd end up regretting. They'd been doing this dance for twenty-four years.

When Alice couldn't take the buzzing any longer, her fingers itching to tear her hair out of its elaborate crown braid, she pulled over. The car bumped off the smooth bitumen onto the loose dirt and gravel, and Alice killed the engine.

Silence—blissful nothingness—surrounded her. She threw the door open. The dusky coolness of the mid-April evening settled against her bare legs. Her phone lit up again, her brother's big brown eyes and watermelon-sized grin appearing. Her finger hovered over the accept icon. Maybe if she told him she was fine, her family would leave her be? Dougie was also the least likely to say, "I told you so". He'd think it, sure, but he wouldn't verbalise the thought, something neither of her parents was capable of. And if he did say something, his boyfriend Rico would be there to run interference.

Alice answered the video call with a heavy sigh. "Hey."

"Thank God!" Rico crowed, pushing Dougie out of the shot. "Where are you? Are you okay? Obviously, you're not okay. That asshole ..."

"I'm ..." Alice's puffy, red eyes were still dangerously close to sad-clown territory.

"Come over. We'll eat carbs, drink an appropriately dry white wine and plot Fuckface's demise," Rico said.

"You think I could talk to my sister?" Dougie reappeared on the screen. "I've spoken to Mum and Dad. They've got a plan."

No surprises there.

"And I'd be happy to help you get a divorce. All free of charge for my favourite sister, of course," Dougie said.

Alice rolled her eyes. She was his only sister. Telling her brother, the mega-successful lawyer, just what a train wreck she was didn't appeal. She looked out across the vast, open plains. Some distance right now was a good idea. "I need a few days. To figure out what I'm going to do. And be alone."

"No, Alley Cat." Dougie was busting out the big guns using Alice's childhood nickname, ignoring that she'd always hated it. Who wants to be called something that skulks around dark places filled with rubbish? "Let us handle this for you. Please? You know Mum and Dad will feel better if they can help."

If Alice had a dollar for every time she'd done something to make someone else happy, she'd never have been tempted to make the bad decision that led to this mess in the first place.

"We'll make sure you're protected. Is your laptop handy? Can you flick me all your financial information?"

She could imagine Dougie's face if he saw her and Phoenix's bank statements. But first, she'd have to know how to access them. They'd lived an extravagant lifestyle, and that shit wasn't cheap. Not that she'd ever really paid much attention to it. Alice had always been allergic to details.

"I just need a few days to get my head together."

As soon as she hung up, her phone rang again. Phoenix's haunting blue eyes replaced her brother's face, and she tossed her mobile onto the dash.

Pushing out of her seat, despite the protest from her heavy limbs and heart, Alice squinted across the fields scattered with gum trees, weathered sheds that slumped sideways and feeding troughs. Soon night would swallow the dusty ground and the property fences made from wooden posts with rows of wire strung between them.

Alice shivered, rubbing her arms. Now everyone knew about all the lies, she'd have to be honest. Admit she went along with it. The thought of confessing the truth made her stomach twist, and she sucked her bottom lip into her mouth, smeared lipstick be damned. Her carefully curated appearance suddenly seemed so trivial ... so *stupid*. Her fitted top sprinkled with tiny sequins was as much of a joke as she was. She should put on a pair of jeans and a plain shirt. And Alice never felt like wearing jeans and a plain shirt, even if it was organic cotton. Well, maybe organic cotton with a sweet flutter sleeve. But the sleeve would have to be *really* cute. She'd always been so careful about making sure the Alice Aspinall everyone saw was the one she desperately wanted to be. Which was no help now that everything had gone to hell.

A large green road sign for Wattle Junction stood out like a beacon, and Alice smoothed her hands over her tutu skirt, pulled at a loose thread and bent over to wipe the road dust off her favourite rose gold brogues. Now the initial adrenaline dump was behind her, all she wanted to do was sleep. Wattle Junction it was, then.

Once she was buckled back in, she ignored the low battery warning on her phone and a quick internet search revealed there were rooms available at the Wattle Junction

Hotel. Two minutes later, she had the skeleton of a plan and a booking confirmation thanks to her parents' emergency credit card.

Alice turned the key in the ignition, and the car clicked once ... twice ... before the engine whimpered pitifully and died. She thumped her hands against the steering wheel. What else could go wrong?

She'd have to call Rico, beg him to drive all the way out here to rescue her and then not tell Dougie. Another Google News alert flashed up on her phone, and Alice froze.

Married Rockstar Live Streams Sex Fest with Mistress.

Her finger hovered above the link, and then her phone died.

As the sun dipped below the horizon, the last bit of colour leaching from the day, Alice threw her car door open and screamed at the sky.

It was all over, and it was all her fault.

THE REALITY of Us will be released on 13 December 2023.

Order your copy here.

ABOUT THE AUTHOR

Emma Mugglestone is a Queenslander who lives in Melbourne, Australia with her family and dogs. When she's not writing contemporary romances filled with small town charm and swoony characters, she can be found chasing sunrises, binge reading rom-coms like it's an Olympic sport and trying to remember her passwords.

Connect with Emma at www.emmamugglestone.com

Also by Emma Mugglestone:

The Wattle Junction Series
The Reality of Us (Book 1, Available 13.12.23)
The Story of Us (Book 2, Available June 2024)

Anthologies:
Anyone But Him (Finding Home, Jawson Ranch Book 1)
All I Want For Chris-mas (Finding Christmas, Jawson Ranch Book 2)

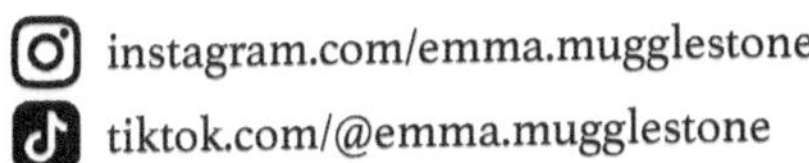

ACKNOWLEDGMENTS

Wattle It Be? is the little novella that I never planned to write but I'm so glad I did. Lots of people have helped me share this story with the world and I'm so grateful.

It wouldn't exist without Cindy Ras, my wonderful cover designer. I randomly saw one of her covers online and knew immediately that I wanted her to design a bearded, tattooed guy who wanted the one woman he couldn't have. And holy moly, did Cindy deliver. I couldn't love how Wyatt and Billie turned out more. It was—literally—the most fun writing prompt I've ever had.

So many wonderful writing friends beta read this story and provided invaluable feedback. They also brighten my days with hilarious group chats and encouragement when I need it. Thank you to Stephanie Hazeltine, Alison Middleton, Elouise Tynan, Holly Brunnbauer, Renae Black, Carrie Clarke, Karen Lieversz and Antonella Licciardi.

My editor, Mel from Write on Editorial, who helped make the story shine.

Special thanks to my family who are the absolute best things to ever happen to me.

My final thanks is to you, the reader. Welcoming you into Wattle Junction has truly been a pleasure and I hope you visit again soon.